Acquittal

By the same author

THE HARD HIT
SQUARE DANCE
DEATH OF A BIG MAN
LANDSCAPE WITH VIOLENCE

ACQUITTAL

JOHN WAINWRIGHT

ST. MARTIN'S PRESS
NEW YORK

CHAPTER ONE

As I walk down the steps, I almost pass out. I wobble a little, and the warder, who is following me, bends forward and touches my upper arm, as if to catch me as I go. I shake his fingers free and take a lungful of air—deep and chest-expanding—in an effort to chase the galloping horses from my brain. It works. The spinning sensation goes away, and I take the last half-dozen steps without swaying.

Those damn steps!

Thirteen of them. The number is very appropriate. Thirteen stone steps, leading from bridewell cells, beneath the Crown Court, up to the dock. And I've walked up and down those steps, twice each day, since Monday. Four days ... it is now Thursday. Eight ascents into purgatory, followed by seven descents into a minor hell.

And now, one descent (the final descent) into freedom. Even the bridewell smells a little sweeter.

Twenty-four hours ago, I hadn't a chance. The D.P.P. counsel had me cold. Hands holding the lapels of his gown, wig slightly askew, he'd itemised every last ounce of evidence against me. He'd systematically wiped every hint of doubt from the faces of those ten men and two women.

Quietly. Without histrionics. Almost apologetically. He'd shown what advocacy means. What the word 'prosecution' means. He'd stretched me on a forensic slab, and he'd slit me wide open.

I'd listened, I'd watched and I'd been absolutely *sure*.

Twenty-four hours ago, I hadn't a chance.

I'd resigned myself—to what? ... twenty years? Behind

a deadpan face, I'd prepared myself for a twenty stretch. I'd been ready for it. I'd *expected* it.

And my man?

To me, it seemed, he'd built bricks, with very little straw. Puny bricks. A tiny cluster of crumbling stones, with which to oppose the cloud-high edifice of the prosecution.

I hadn't a chance ... twenty-four hours ago.

But (less than ten minutes ago) that jury pulled the perfect loaves-and-fishes conjuring trick. 'Not Guilty' ... on a majority verdict. Ten and two. Ten of them had found doubt which even *I* couldn't see. Doubt which had dragged a quick frown of displeasure from the old man wearing scarlet and ermine.

Somebody in that jury room must have done some very persuasive arguing.

And the two who wouldn't be budged?

The two who were out-voted?

I am suddenly very curious. I have watched those faces every day, for four days. I know them. Correction ... I *thought* I knew them. I thought I knew their verdict, before the verdict was given, but I was wrong.

But not wholly wrong.

Two of them have remained constant. Two of them have reached the conclusion I would have reached.

Which two?

My guess is, the women. My guess is, that the men leaned a little in my direction, and were prepared to be talked into mercy, but that the two women dug in their heels, and refused to be budged. And who can blame them? They had facts on their side. Evidence. And women stick together, and this four-day war of words has been fought across the corpse of a murdered woman.

So-o, my guess is, that the two women jurors identified themselves with Lissa, and wanted vengeance in her name. Vengeance. Not, necessarily, law. And vengeance leaves little room for doubt, and no room at all for mercy.

I'm almost sure, but I'm still curious. I'd like to know ... which of the twelve jurors hungered after my hide?

My guess is, the women.

'Your things?'

'Eh?' I jerk my mind from thoughts of steps, and jurors, and near-miracles.

The warder uses a deliberately couldn't-care-less tone of voice.

He says, 'Your personal effects, Russell. Shaving gear. Toothbrush. Your ...'

'Would you mind putting "mister" in front of my name?' I ask, mildly.

'... wallet and its contents. Do you want to come back to the prison, to collect them? Or shall we forward them?'

It is a knack they have. It annoys me, but I have already grown accustomed to it. You exist, only if they *decree* that you exist. My interruption didn't even make him pause in his monologue. I doubt if he even heard it. He has certain things to say. He says them. Then, when what he has to say amounts to a direct question, he acknowledges the presence of the man to whom he is speaking. The knack goes with the uniform, the uniform goes with the job, and the job is the most dehumanising employment ever to disguise itself as a 'vocation'.

The non-human looks at me, with expressionless eyes, and says, 'Well?'

I say, 'Keep them. Send them to a jumble-sale. If I ever need a used toothbrush, I'll let you know.'

The warder nods his head. Once. God knows how many times he's had this, or a similar, remark made to him in such circumstances. He is beyond anger and beyond out-rage. He is beyond all normal feeling. He notes my reaction to his officially required question ... then forgets me.

Another relevant thought pushes its way to the surface. That, compared with this man, I am lucky.

7

That, today—and every day, until he reaches his elder years—this man will return to H.M. Prison. That, voluntarily, he has accepted a sentence few courts would inflict ... and without having committed a crime.

I feel a flash of pity for this man, and his kind.

And now, I don't know what to do. Do I walk away? Do I stroll down the corridor, between the cells, and ask the uniformed guardian at the door to turn the key, and allow me my freedom? Is it as easy as that? What the hell do I do *next*?

I take my mac from the bench, alongside the wall. Very slowly, I thread my arms through the sleeves. I settle the shoulders into position, and begin to fasten the buttons.

I take my time. Slow-motion.

What the hell do I do *next*?

There are warders around. There are policemen around. I could ask. But, to ask would be a sign of weakness. It would be a minor defeat, after a glorious victory.

Everybody ignores me. The warders—the policemen—busy themselves with their puny authorities. They prepare prisoners for the dock. They escort prisoners to cells. They fill in forms. They go about their work, and pretend I am not here.

Deliberately?

Possibly ... but, possibly, because I am no longer their concern.

These men deal in guilt. They deal in prison, and accusation. An acquittal is a state of affairs beyond their professional ken. I have been acquitted, therefore I am not of their world. Therefore I do not exist. Therefore I am no longer their concern.

And (damn it!) they're right. I'm *not* their concern.

I am a free man. I am as free as any pedestrian walking the street, beyond the confines of this court-house.

I am Harvey Russell. I have been accused of a hideous crime. But I have been acquitted. Therefore, I am free.

8

They have no right to ... to ... to ...

The door, at the end of the corridor, opens and a human being I know enters the cell area.

Six weeks ago (just before the committal proceedings) I hated this man. He was my enemy. His sworn duty was to put me behind bars; to cage me, like a rogue animal, unfit to roam free amongst its fellows. He worked hard at it, too. Objectivity. He would have argued that he had no personal axe to grind, when he arrested me. He would have argued that he was merely a 'collector of evidence'.

The various ways, in which men delude themselves!

There is nothing impersonal about being *charged* with murder. There is damn all objectivity when you're being arrested.

At that moment, you loathe the man who represents society's revenge. At that moment, you hate him and you truly believe you'll continue to hate him, beyond your last heartbeat.

More delusions.

You're wrong ... you don't.

I don't hate him, now.

He comes towards me, and I greet him with a half-smile of welcome. Not because I like him. (Although, God knows, I don't *dis*like him ... not even that.) But, because I *know* him. He is not a stranger. I have conversed with him, in the past, and he has treated me as an equal.

'Groggy?' he asks.

'No.'

'No?'

'Just a little ...'

'You look it. You look like a case of delayed shock.'

'A little,' I agree, reluctantly. 'I—er ...'

'Haven't you got used to the idea yet?'

'Something like that.'

'The news-hawks are waiting,' he warns.

'Oh!'

'I thought I'd come down, and let you know.'

'Oh!'

'One last Harvey Russell front-page splurge.'

I say, 'Oh!' again. Mainly because I can think of nothing else to say.

'There's a back way out,' he suggests. 'It's your choice, but ...'

'I'd like that.'

'Good.' He pats his pockets, then adds, 'Cigarette?'

'Please. They—er—they wouldn't let me ...'

'I know.' He grins a quick, lop-sided grin. 'Her Majesty's Prisons. They aren't geared to handle "innocent" men.'

The way he says it leaves no room for doubt. It matters not what some putty-brained jury said. It matters not what the record shows. 'Clean sheets' are not on the agenda. Harvey Russell murdered his wife—and was lucky enough to get away with it ... and *that* is the verdict of the police, as conveyed by Detective Chief Inspector Tim Crawford.

But, you win some—you lose some ... and no hard feelings.

Without putting it into words, Crawford passes the message, as he opens the slide of the cigarette packet, then lights my cigarette before he lights his own.

The door at the end of the cell corridor opens again. This time, it is Braithwaite, the solicitor. He is here to congratulate. Possibly to advise. Without changing his expression, he could, equally well, commiserate ... he has that sort of face.

Nevertheless, he is a good solicitor.

He looks questioningly at Crawford, and says, 'I didn't expect to find you here, chief inspector.'

'No?' Crawford casually flicks the conversational ball back into Braithwaite's court.

'You heard the verdict, of course?'

'Of course.'

I stand back, and watch these two spar. It is a minor education in civilised combat; something I have witnessed before—during the murder investigation—and always with the same result. A dignified backing-down by Braithwaite.

Braithwaite is a fully qualified solicitor. He is a commissioner for oaths, and holds the degree of LL.B.(Lond). He should be a match for any policeman. Indeed, he *is* a match for any *other* policeman. But (even paper qualification for paper qualification) he falls short of Crawford. Crawford is not merely a detective chief inspector, he is a very *special* detective chief inspector. To the best of my knowledge, he is the only working policeman, in the United Kingdom, qualified to slip the letters Ph.D. behind his name. He is not only Detective Chief Inspector Crawford, he is also *Doctor* Crawford ... if he cares to demand his full rank, name and title.

Crawford is unique. He marries academic cunning with practical guile, and the mix is almost unbeatable. Braithwaite can't beat it ... although he's tried hard enough. And he still tries.

He turns to me, and says, 'Mr Russell, if you've suffered any form of harassment, since you left the dock ...'

'Mr Braithwaite.' Crawford's smile carries gentle mockery. 'If that's the best you can do ...'

'Have you, Mr Russell?'

I have the impression that Braithwaite is praying for an affirmative answer.

'No harassment,' I say.

'You're sure?'

'I'm sure. The other thing, in fact. The chief inspector came down to warn me about the waiting press.'

'Oh! I—er ...'

I say, 'Thanks for coming down, Braithwaite. And thanks for all you've done ... tell defending counsel I'm grateful. I'll meet your bill, the day it arrives.'

'I ...' For a fraction of a second Braithwaite's face shows

an expression. Annoyance. Then, he says, 'In that case, I'll leave.'

He has cause for annoyance. He, and the defending counsel, have just handed me twenty years of unexpected freedom and, to be so offhanded—so churlish—is to be an ungrateful bastard. It's what I am—or, what I sound to be ... an ungrateful bastard. But it was Braithwaite's job and, when the reckoning comes, he will demand a high fee ... and I am at the tail-end of four of the roughest days of my life.

At this moment, I haven't time to waste on unnecessary gratitude.

Braithwaite nods a brief farewell to Crawford and walks back towards the door of the cell area.

Crawford draws his cigarette a couple of times, then says, 'When you're ready.'

'I'm more than that. I'm waiting.'

We leave the warders and the policemen—the cell area and the stone steps leading up to the dock—and, about a hundred yards and a few dozen twists and turns of corridors later, I breathe God's good air, as a free man.

And never let the environment fanatics fool you. It is still that ... *good* air.

CHAPTER TWO

It is, perhaps, odd. It is, perhaps, illogical.

That, here am I—Harvey Russell, the wife-killer who, for the last few weeks, has been glowering from front pages throughout the land—rounding off a good meal, having just eaten that meal in the company of the man ordained by the public to put me behind prison walls.

It is odd—it is illogical ... and yet it is neither odd nor illogical. Not if you know Tim Crawford. Not if you know him as I know him.

I should hate him, but I don't hate him ... partly, because he refuses to *be* hated.

We have reached the coffee-and-cigarette stage of the meal.

I ease half an inch of ash into the ash-tray, and say, 'Crawford, they should pickle your brain.'

His expression is one of mild interest in the proposition.

I say, 'When you're gone, they should pickle your brain, for posterity. It's a one-off job.'

He waits for whatever explanations might be forthcoming. He waits. He is a great one for 'waiting'. He has patience ... an endless capacity for patience. They tell me Sioux Indians have this never-ending patience. If so, Crawford should be made an honorary member of the tribe.

He even *looks* a little like a North American Indian. The high cheek bones. The slightly narrowed, slightly suspicious, slightly laughing eyes. Dark eyes, which drop an impregnable curtain of mild mockery between the outside world and his thoughts. The eyes of a born poker-player.

And the mouth. Thin-lipped and, if the tilt didn't give the hint of quirky humour to the sardonic laughter of the eyes, the word 'cruel' might spring to mind. A slit of a mouth, but without the streak of sadism which usually goes with such a mouth.

And the man, himself? The overall impression?

'Lean and hungry'—that, perhaps ... but not 'lean and aggressive'. Not 'lean and *angry*'. He is not an obviously 'angry' man, although I do not doubt that he can be driven to anger. A cold and terrible anger. But, a controlled and well-directed anger ... and God help the recipient of that anger!

13

'Are you married?' I ask and, for the life of me, I don't know why I ask the question.

He shakes his head.

'No ... you wouldn't be.'

'Nor are you ... now,' he observes, mildly.

'Or ever again.'

'As bad as that?'

I say, 'You made the enquiries.'

'True.'

'You needed a motive. You found what you were looking for.'

He moves one shoulder in a tiny shrug of acquiescence.

I sigh, then murmur, 'Even so, you wouldn't know.'

'No?'

'Not being married ... you wouldn't know.'

'Tell me,' he suggests.

'You asked around. You made all the necessary enquiries. All those witnesses. They must have told you *something*.'

'Ah, but not *you*.'

'No,' I agree.

'Not you,' he repeats, gently.

I say, 'My plea was "Not Guilty". You needed motive ... to back means, and opportunity.'

'We needed motive,' he agrees.

'I wasn't foolish enough to give you motive, on a plate.'

'Quite.' He nods quiet, but complete understanding.

The waiter moves in, to top up the coffee. I wave him aside, but Crawford pushes his cup and saucer a fraction of an inch, across the table-cloth, in a gesture of assent. The waiter pours fresh coffee into Crawford's cup. Black, strong coffee, which Crawford sips unsweetened.

The waiter moves out of earshot.

Crawford sips, and smokes ... and waits.

I tell him.

Why not? Ten of my peers have decided in my favour. Although I didn't know it, I was a five-to-one-on favourite.

I romped home ... well clear of the field. I can now afford to be magnanimous to the loser. Especially as he is such a *good* loser. No bitterness. No half-hearted excuses. Crawford is the sort of loser who deserves magnanimity.

I talk in a low voice; a voice which carries as far as Crawford, but not as far as the adjoining table.

I say, 'Lissa was a bitch. A bitch, on perpetual heat ... but I don't have to tell you that, do I?'

He bends his lips into an encouraging smile, but says nothing.

I continue, 'That much you could prove. Or, some of it. Enough. Enough to establish a motive. That she had men. That they shared her bed. That I was her husband. Ergo ... jealousy. Ergo ... motive.'

'Ergo ... motive,' he murmurs.

I say, 'My friend, I wish it had been as simple as *that*. As uncomplicated as *that*.'

'Really?'

'She had men. Many men. Don't ask me how many. I didn't "lose count". I stopped counting. I stopped caring.'

'I see.'

I watch his face, as I say, 'But that was something you didn't underline ... right?'

'Not caring.' He smiles a slight smile of admission. 'Evidence of "not caring" might have weakened evidence of motive.'

'Not too much. Not too little.'

'Measured. Just the right amount,' he agrees.

'But, you were wrong.'

'You have facts on your side, Russell.' He sighs a mock sigh. 'An acquittal. That proves we were wrong.'

'Totally wrong,' I correct him. 'Not merely wrong, in degree. Wrong on the whole issue of motive.'

'Really?' He raises interested eyebrows.

'Sex,' I say. 'Forget it.'

The eyebrows lift a little higher.

I say, 'That's the weakness of a police investigation, Crawford. Policemen have very basic minds. Man kills woman—woman kills man ... there's only one motive, as far as the police are concerned.'

'It often is,' he says, softly.

'Sometimes. Not this time.'

'No?' A slight tilt of the quizzical eyebrows calls me a liar.

'I don't need sex,' I say.

He doesn't reply.

I drain my coffee until the dregs touch my lips, then I lower the cup onto its saucer. I take a long, deep drag on my cigarette.

I say, 'That's one thing I do *not* need ... sex.'

'Fifty-two,' he muses. 'A healthy, male homo sapiens ... and you don't need sex?'

'Take it, or leave it,' I correct myself.

'That's not quite the same thing.'

'More, or less.'

'Oh, no.' He shakes his head gently. 'Not even that. The prison psychologist ...'

'What the hell do *they* know?'

'He wouldn't tell you how to build houses.'

'Nut doctors!'

'Like you, they're professionals. They can spot a queer at ten miles. Even a suppressed queer.'

'So?'

'You're normal, Russell. You have no hang-ups. So-o ... forgive me. But don't feed me a no-sex-please line of chat. You need it. Like every other fully-fledged man.'

'All right,' I say, softly. Tightly. 'I need sex. *When* I need sex, I buy it. It's a commodity. For sale, over a counter. For sale, on a bed. Pick a hole, use it then pay your money ... then, forget it.'

'It's a philosophy,' he smiles.

16

'Indeed. It's a very down-to-earth philosophy. A very practical philosophy. It *works*.'

Crawford tastes his coffee. He lowers the cup, and smokes his cigarette. He watches my face, and there is mockery in his expression; mockery, but without contempt, dances at his mouth corners.

He says, 'Fine ... we were wrong about the motive.'

'Totally wrong.'

'Okay,' he coaxes, 'what?'

I need no coaxing.

I say, 'Greed.'

'Simple greed.' He clicks his tongue, in soft, self-disgust. 'As basic as that. Simple greed ... and we missed it.'

'Complicated greed. Complicated enough to need an accountant to spot it. A greed that started as an uncomfortable feeling—no more than that ... a feeling that something was wrong. Something was a little too involved ... but, at the same time, a little too smooth and fast. Something I didn't understand. A feeling ... a very uncomfortable feeling. A nagging.'

'You're hinting at fraud.' He sounds genuinely surprised.

'It needed checking. So, I checked it.'

'I see.'

'With an independent accountant.'

He repeats, 'I see,' softly ... then waits.

I squash my cigarette into the ash-tray. I lean forward, and closer to the table. I try to get across to him what I am anxious for him to hear. Anxious for him to understand. All I want him to know, but not too much ... not enough to cause him to draw wrong conclusions. I choose my words carefully. I speak them slowly.

I say, 'Everybody's greedy, Crawford. You—me ... everybody! We're all greedy for something. Most of us deny it. I think greed is a fault impossible to identify in yourself. A fault nobody admits. But a universal fault. We all covet *something*. Money. Possessions. Authority. Social standing. *Something*. We're all greedy, Crawford. Every last one of us.'

I pause and, into the pause, Crawford slips a question. 'Your wife? She was greedy ... right?'

'Right.' I nod.

'Which, by your own argument, means she wasn't unique.'

'With Lissa,' I say, 'it was a disease. Everything! She wanted the world, and she wanted to be queen of the world. Basically, she didn't know what the hell she *did* want. As a wife she was impossible. As a partner in the firm, she was a sick joke.'

'You mentioned fraud,' he murmurs.

'Nothing specific ... not yet. I hadn't time.'

'Before ...' He hesitates, then says, 'Before she died?'

'Before she was murdered.' I meet him, eye for eye, and say, 'Don't be coy, Crawford. She was murdered ... remember? Before she was murdered.'

He nods, slowly. As if pondering what I have already said. As if using my voiced suspicions for new thoughts.

I say, 'Lissa. We shared. Everything. Even after the break-up of our marriage ... it was still fifty-fifty. We had a joint account. Any day of the week, she could have written out a four-figure cheque.'

'Joint account? Even after a divorce?' He sounds surprised.

'It's not illegal.'

'No. But ...'

'So why not? I—er ...' I suddenly feel embarrassed. Awkward. I mutter, 'Divorce, or not, I still counted her as my wife. I still felt responsible for her. That bloody divorce. I didn't want it ... separation would have been enough. Without dragging the law into things.'

'Mutual agreement?' he asks, with a smile.

'Why not? It would have worked.'

'Really?'

'The firm ... her signature carried as much weight as mine. Or Bill's. Or Vi's.'

'Sir William Macks? And Lady Violet Macks?'

Instead of answering empty questions, I continue, 'Lissa —my wife ... she worshipped money. Money ... not wealth. She loved the feel of the stuff through her fingers. She parted with it, reluctantly. Almost as if it was a physical pain. Money—Bank of England notes and silver coins ... they were her only gods.'

'A miser?' He allows a flickering smile to brush his lips, then says, 'You mean she was a miser?'

I light a fresh cigarette as I answer, and my answer is an oblique answer ... because a straightforward answer is impossible.

I say, 'She also possessed things. She gave nothing away. Nothing! If it was hers, it usually stayed hers. That, or it doubled—sometimes tripled—its value ... merely because it had *been* hers. She sold things. Sometimes ... not often, but sometimes. She never gave things away but, sometimes, she sold them ... and, always, at her own ridiculously exaggerated price.

'The same with social standing. She claimed the top shelf ... and alone!'

My voice has gradually become louder, as my disgust for this wife of mine is transformed into words. I steady myself, draw on the cigarette, and lower my voice.

I say, 'Time was—y'know ... when we were younger. When we were first married. She could have had the world. And the sun, and the stars, to place alongside it. Everything! Anything! If she asked, she got. But—believe me, Crawford—she didn't know *what* she wanted ... only that, having got it, she wanted more. Or something else. She was never satisfied. Never! She was never grateful ... never content.'

There is a silence. Crawford, too, lights a new cigarette; he chain-lights it from the one he has just finished, then

thumbs the dead butt cold into the base of the ash-tray ...
then waits for whatever else I am going to say, knowing
that, having said this much, there must be a rounding-off.
There must be a conclusion.

My voice is slightly hoarse, as I say, 'Crawford, I'm a
bricky. Basically, that's what I am—that's my trade ... a
bricklayer. I know the firm—"R. & M."—means I'm supposed to be something special. Big business ... somebody
better than the rest. But, I'm not. I'm still a bricky, at
heart. I'm basic. What education I have, I've picked up
on the way. Self-educated. Self-made. Self-taught. And that
means I lack the diplomacy of the well-learned. It means
I know how to hate. And I howl, when I'm hurt ... I
howl, and I hit back. I don't turn the other cheek. And
I know when I've had enough. I know when I've had a
gutful ... and, at that point, I take no more.'

'At that point,' says Crawford, casually, 'you kill.'

I pick my words very carefully.

I say, 'At that point, I *could* kill.'

'Ah, yes ... but do you? Could you? *Have* you?'

'No ... according to a recent verdict.'

He smiles his twisted smile across the table at me.

He murmurs, 'You're safe now, Russell.'

'Safe?'

'It really *is* the law. It's no fairy tale. You've been found
"Not Guilty" ... and you stay "Not Guilty". Sell the why,
and how, to some Sunday newsrag ... you're still "Not
Guilty". Double-jeopardy isn't part of the English Legal
System.'

I lift my napkin from my knees and drop it onto the
side-plate.

'You're safe,' he repeats, softly.

I say, 'Thanks for the meal, Crawford.'

'My pleasure.'

'I have things to do.'

'Of course.' Then, as I turn to go, he adds, 'You wouldn't like to tell me?'

I face him again. Look down at him. Weigh the pros and the cons ... those thousands of pros and cons!

The clincher?

The realisation that this man, Crawford, has screwed himself into the ground, for almost eight weeks. Probably much longer. Non-stop ... and for what?

For *nothing*!

To listen to a crack-brained jury gum up the whole works.

And yet, he bears no outward sign of bitterness. No obvious grudge. He shields me from the newsmen. He takes me to a good restaurant. He buys me a fine meal ... the first civilised meal I've tasted for weeks.

Policeman—whatever he is—this man has class. He has a certain flair ... a certain style. He deserves *something*.

I say, 'This double-jeopardy thing. You wouldn't con me?'

'My oath.' The lopsided smile continues to smile up at me. 'You could go back into that court. You could try to change your plea. You could try to plead "Guilty" ... and they wouldn't listen. You're innocent, Russell. The law may be many things. Involved. Slow. Foolish. Many things ... but it's always certain. *You're innocent.*'

I believe him.

I take a deep breath.

Then, I say, 'Okay. I killed her. I shot her ... three times, with the .22. I sloshed a mixture of petrol and paraffin around, then struck a match. You've worked hard for that confession, Crawford. You have it, now ... for what it's worth.'

CHAPTER THREE

I drive the Stag, hard. I have many things to do—many calls to make—and I am not too certain how much time I have. Not too *much* time. Since that unexpected verdict, a lot of people will have moved. Fast! The big cover-up operation will have been launched ... and there *has* to be a cover-up. Telephone messages will have been sent. Hurried meetings will have been arranged. A dozen cats will be already causing panic in the dove-cote.

Which is as it should be.

Which, with corruption, it always *is!*

Corruption is like a cancer. It grows, in all directions ... up, sideways and down. And in all directions, at the same time. Nobody can pull a major building-contract con trick, without other men being in the know. A *lot* of other men. A lot of underlings must know—or must, at least, have guessed—and those underlings must also know that knowledge, plus silence, makes a man as guilty as the scoundrels at the top.

Already, a lot of people will have been smoothed. A lot of people will have been paid. But more—many more ... and it will take time, and persuasion.

But I don't know how much time.

I only know that I have shortened that time, by dropping the hint to Crawford ... that it is now a race, between Crawford, and me.

A race which I am determined to win.

I therefore drive the Stag, hard, from Colbank police station—where it has been housed, for the last few weeks —and towards Yew Cottage. I drive automatically, and the car answers my responses, like the thoroughbred it is, and my mind is free to ask itself questions ... and, in part, to straighten itself on its gimbals.

The question. The big—Everest-sized—question.

Why the confession? Why, after weeks of denial, switch to a sudden George Washington state of mind? Damn it to hell ... *why*?

Because I now have this double-jeopardy safety-net?

That has to be one reason. But not the only reason. There are other reasons. And reasons for reasons. And even reasons for *those* reasons.

Like railway-lines converging onto a major terminus, all these reasons move in, and concentrate upon a single name.

Lissa ...

I drive the Stag through the late afternoon country lanes. Hood open, and the overhead slipstream ruffling my hair. It is an experience I had resigned myself to merely remembering ... but, instead, it is *now*. It is a present blessing, and not a remembered dream. It is not —as I had expected—a memory, to be treasured and burnished in some prison cell.

Therefore, why can't that be enough? Why can't that be *enough*?

Lissa ...

Because this is *now*. Because the last few weeks are *then*. The tense makes the difference. The past is past ... and a prolonged nightmare. If memory can be blacked out, the past will be forgotten ... if memory *can* be blacked out.

Lissa ...

The half-madness of a prison cell is conducive to strange thoughts. It makes for a crazy, ice-cold logic. Clinical, in its disregard of normal convention and accepted standards.

Murderers, for example. Killers. Killers are often very nondescript people. Man-in-the-street-type people. So-o—

all God's children are killers ... if pushed too far. The logic insists upon the rightness of this proposition. The killer can never be identified, before his crime. The killer is you—the killer is me—the killer is *anybody*.

But, the victim?

What about the *victim*?

Cell-thoughts have brought me to a firm conclusion. That there are men, and women, who are born murder victims. That, to know them is to identify them. That, to know them is to know that, if they don't alter their ways, they'll drive some poor devil beyond the limit of self-control. The elastic will break. The crime will be committed—they'll be shot, or strangled, or stabbed ... and then it will be too late.

These people are born for a violent end.

Like Lissa.

Lissa ... and the gentle insanity of a prison remand cell.

A reason for the confession, perhaps? An indirect explanation to Crawford?

Crawford is no fool. He needs nothing spelling out. A hint is enough; a verbal cryptograph. It was a confession, but it was also much more than a confession. It was something of which Crawford should be made aware. That it takes two people to commit the crime of murder; that it requires a killer, and a victim, and that each must contribute his, or her, share to the commission of that crime.

And more ...

That, often, each is equally at fault but, more often than not, the blame—the condemnation—is unequally apportioned. Speak no ill of the dead. But, why not? The dead—even the violently dead—do not become sanctified, by reason of their death; they are not deserving of new sympathy—a sympathy undeserved in life—merely because they are dead.

Lissa ...

24

The Stag takes the country lanes, at a steady fifty—bends and all—and the slipstream ruffles my hair and, as I drive, I ask myself questions ... impossible questions which, at this moment, do not admit of answers.

CHAPTER FOUR

Thirty minutes later, I brake the Stag to a halt at the gate of Yew Cottage.

The men are packing up for the day. The labourers are hosing down the concrete mixer, stacking the fallen bricks, collecting the debris of stone chippings and joist and floorboard off-cuts. The bricklayers are cleaning their trowels and chisels. The masons are putting the last touches to the pointing, between the day's stonework. The plasterers are sluicing and drying their floats. Bob Garret is collecting his saws, his set-squares, his hammers, and returning them to his tool-box.

It is the end of a working day.

It brings back memories ...

Long-gone, and almost misplaced, memories ...

Memories of stretching back, neck and shoulder muscles after a hard day's graft. Memories of the 'sing' of a good trowel against the surface of brickwork; of squeezed-out mortar, sliced off and picked up in a single, automatic sweep of the right hand, as the left hand reaches for the next brick. Memories of a 'feel' ... the 'feel' of a good, well-built wall. Memories of a knowledge; the warm knowledge that a wall is plumb and level, even before the bubble in the spirit gives verification of that knowledge.

Memories of a craftsman; a craftsman who's done it so

many times, and done it *well* so many times, that errors are rare enough to be discounted.

Tormenting memories of simple, uncluttered pleasures; of an uncomplicated happiness which, at the time, was grossly under-valued.

The men see me, as I walk towards the door of the cottage. Their glances are almost surreptitious. Surprise—something not too far from shock—widens their eyes for a moment, before they deliberately return to their work. One of them nods a greeting ... then jerks, as if guilty of an unintended sin, before turning his back.

I understand.

I shouldn't *be* here.

I should have been convicted. I should, by this time, be back behind the walls of a prison and, that I am not, is an affront to their simple belief in British justice.

They are good men. Hand-picked ... and, by me. Even the labourers, in their own way, are artisans. The 'Lump' system has never posed problems for Russell and Macks, Limited. Nor have we ever had serious union trouble. From the first, we've demanded the best ... and we've been prepared to pay for the best. Every tradesman is fully apprentice-trained, and most of them have City and Guild qualifications with which to back their expertise. No skimping of materials, or short-cuts in an effort to save time. What we've built, we've built to last ... always! And, via what we've built, we've built a reputation.

That reputation has been built upon the broad backs of good men. Honest men. Responsible, and respected, men.

If only marriage could also be built upon the backs of such men ... and, if possible, without women!

I allow myself the luxury of a long, deep sigh and walk into the cottage.

Bob Garret has entered the cottage. He is concentrating his attention upon the task of honing the blade of a wood-chisel upon the concave surface of a well-used oil-stone; slow, light-pressured strokes and, after every half-dozen strokes, or so, wiping the blade with oil-stained cheese-cloth and testing the cutting edge with the ball of his thumb.

So many times—so many *hundreds* of times—I've watched Garret doing the same thing, at the end of a day's work. All my life ... as far back as I can remember. He'll go on forever; every day, for eternity, perfecting an already perfect tool. If he stops—if he misses one day—the universe will cease to spin, and will explode into blazing nothingness.

Garret worked for my father, when the firm was Henry Russell & Son; when the work-force ran to only one chippy ... Bob Garret. Garret taught me the inner secrets of top-class workmanship; gruffly spoken words of wisdom; words as sacred today as they were so many years back.

'The tools, lad. Make sure they're good, make sure they're balanced and make sure they fit your hand. Keep 'em that way, and don't use 'em on cheap material. Nurse 'em. They're your bread and butter. Then, if you make a complete arse of owt, you'll know where the blame lies.'

Truth—fundamental truth ... reduced to growled advice from a bad-tempered craftsman.

To know where the blame lies, 'if you make a complete arse of anything'.

Marriage, for example?

'Bob,' I say, softly.

'Oh, aye.' He strokes the blade of the chisel once more up, then down, the stone. He raises his head, and says, 'They've let you out, then?'

'Surprised?'

He uses the cheese-cloth, then tests the cutting-edge.

He says, 'I'm past being surprised, these days, lad.'

'An acquittal.'

'Oh, aye?'

'Not guilty.'

'Or maybe they can't prove it.'

He opens the tool-box and places the sharpened chisel carefully—almost reverently—into its allotted place. He wipes the stone clean of oil, with the cheese-cloth.

I glance up at the new joists. At the underside of the new bedroom floorboards.

'The roof timbers?' I ask.

'The fire didn't get that far.'

'Good.'

'You should know.'

'I—er—I suppose ...'

'You watched it being built. To your own specifications.'

'Renovated,' I correct him.

'Gutted,' he contradicts. 'Then, re-built.'

He unties the strings of his apron, then lifts the neck-loop of his apron forward and over his short-cut, grey thatch. He is one of the few carpenters who still wear the uniform of their trade; the heavy white apron, with its wide, deep front pocket. It is one more tiny proof of his jealous pride in his skill in the working of timber. He folds the apron, prior to placing it on top of the tools in the box.

He says, 'Well seasoned oak ... remember?'

I nod.

'It takes more than a match, and a few pints of petrol, to get *that* going.'

Again, I nod.

He closes the lid of the tool-box, then fishes in his trouser pocket for a loaded key-ring. He selects one of the keys, and locks his beloved tools away for the night.

As always, I admire the tool-box itself. Even the tool-box. Planned by Garret, then made by him; with dove-tailed corners, a piano-hinge and a mortice lock any desk would be proud to display. With drawers, and tiny cup-boards, and a carefully positioned housing for each tool and instrument. Nobody could *buy* such a tool-box. Few men could make one.

He returns the key-ring to his pocket.

He says, 'About where you're standing, I reckon.'

'What?'

'Where she was.'

'Oh!'

A slow frown spreads across his face, and he growls, 'Why the hell didn't you just divorce her?'

'That easy?'

Bitterness rides the surface of my counter-question.

'You have the brass,' he says.

I nod.

'And you've had enough cause.'

'Yes.'

'So, why not just divorce her?'

'Bob,' I say, softly. Heavily.

I have a desire to talk. To explain. To seek understanding ... sympathy, perhaps.

I offer him a cigarette, but he makes a grunted refusal. Instead, he does something I have watched him do countless times in the past. He takes a scratched and battered tobacco tin from his pocket and, from it, a length of thin twist. With a bone-handled pocket-knife, whose blade has been honed to a razor's edge, he slices tiny discs of tobacco from the twist. He returns twist, tin and knife to his pocket, then begins to rub the tobacco into shreds. He uses the palm of his left hand and the heel of his right; a slow, rhythmic, pestle-and-mortar movement.

He does me the courtesy of listening, without interruption. He gives me what he would call 'a fair hearing' ... which means he lets me say what I have to say, but without, necessarily, believing me.

I smoke the cigarette, as I talk; punctuating the sentences with inhalations and exhalations of tobacco smoke.

I say, 'I'm like you, Bob. I'm a builder ... like you. And

all the money in the world won't change it. Working-class. You, and me. It's nothing to be ashamed of ... but it's what we *are*. What we'll stay. A mentality. A way of thinking. A set of standards, if you like. And working-class folk don't divorce very easily. Any more than they play polo. Any more than they mess about with debs, and such like.

'Money hasn't a lot to do with it. All money means is that we live in better houses. Eat better food. Wear better clothes. That's all. We don't *think* differently. We can't. We still laugh at the same things ... the same simple, mucky jokes. We don't read different books. Money doesn't suddenly make a man understand what all these long-winded Russian authors are trying to say. We don't even buy different newspapers. We don't buy *The Times*, because we don't like *The Times*. We still stick to the *Mirror* and its cheesecake, and its two-times-two way of putting things.

'The same with divorce. Divorce is for actors, and the like. For the upper-crust. Bricklayers don't divorce. Joiners don't divorce. They stick it out, and stay miserable.

'Working-class. It makes us less than others, in some way. Or, maybe better ... maybe bigger. Maybe stronger. We make a choice, and we stick by it. To hell with the misery. To hell with the consequences. Maybe it makes us better. More honourable. Maybe it means we're weak. More stupid. It's a six-and-two-threes argument. There's no real answer.

'But, this is a fact. Your childhood—your youth—conditions you, for the rest of your life. Yours did. Mine did. You're a chippy, Bob. I'm a bricklayer—and, no matter how much money ... I'm still a bricklayer. And bricklayers don't go in for divorce.'

I wait for his reaction.

I am worried, and peculiarly anxious for his understanding.

He thumbs shredded twist into the bowl of a broken cherry-wood pipe, spins the wheel of a cheap lighter and sucks the flame down onto the surface of the tobacco.

And there is more nostalgia.

The stench of that tobacco—the smell of 'Bob Garret's bloody pipe'—it is as much part of the firm as it is part of my own life.

Dear God ... *more* nostalgia!

'Happens you're right,' he growls, reluctantly.

'I'm right.'

'But, come to that, bricklayers don't go in for murder.'

'The court verdict ...'

'I don't give a sod about the court. Courts can say owt.'

'Nevertheless ...'

'You were a wild bugger, in your younger days.' He scowls disapproval at memories conjured up in his mind. 'I've seen you go for a bloke with a brick-hammer ... more than once. And mean it. You'd a paddy. You still have.'

'Bob!' I plead.

'Unless you've changed ... and I doubt *that*.'

'You're my friend, Bob,' I say, softly. Hoarsely. 'All these years. We've been friends. Workmates. We've been ...'

'No. I wouldn't say "friends".' Garret shakes his head, slowly. 'The gaffer's lad. After that, the gaffer. That's all. Not a bad gaffer ... I'll grant you that. A lot better than some. But—y'know—moody. All your own way, or else ... A bit unpredictable. And with a hell of a temper ... and the position to get away with it. We've put up some fine buildings together. Between us. But never "friends". Not what I'd call "friends" ...'

CHAPTER FIVE

R. v. RUSSELL.
Extract from Record of Trial.
Cross-examination of Accused, by Prosecuting Counsel.
Counsel. Russell, the court has heard evidence of character.
Russell. Yes.
Counsel. Your character.
Russell. Yes.
Counsel. At first glance, evidence of a man of good character.
Russell. Yes, sir. People have been good enough to ...
Counsel. Would you agree with all that's been said?
Russell. I'm sorry. I don't understand the question.
Counsel. These witnesses we've heard. People who claim to know you. All the nice things they've said about you. Do you agree with their assessment of your character?
Russell. It's—er—it's not for me to ...
Counsel. Come now, Russell. Don't be modest. Do you agree with their assessment of you, as a man?
Russell. They know me. Presumably they're ...
Counsel. You misunderstand me, Russell. I am not doubting the honesty of those friends of yours who have come to plead for you. I am asking you a simple question. Knowing yourself, as you do know yourself—as every man knows himself—would you agree with their assessment of you?
Russell. Yes. I think so.
Counsel. As a reasonable, and kindly, man?
Russell. I—I don't know how to answer that question.
Counsel. The court will accept a simple, affirmative answer, Russell.

Russell. It's not as ...

Counsel. Or a simple, negative answer.

Russell. I find it a difficult question to answer.

Counsel. In that case, let me assist you. Do you, or do you not, agree with the witnesses who have been called to give evidence of your good character?

Russell. Yes, I ... I think I agree with them.

Counsel. They have, in effect, described you as a fairly ordinary man ... wouldn't you say?

Russell. Yes.

Counsel. Not a particularly mild man. Not a saint. But not a violent man. Not a man given to excessive violence.

Russell. Yes. Very ordinary.

Counsel. A man with a temper—as most men have tempers —but not a man with an uncontrollable temper.

Russell. An ordinary man.

Counsel. The temper of a man who doesn't suffer fools easily. That sort of temper.

Russell. Yes.

Counsel. Not, of course, a man with the temper of a murderer?

Russell. I'm not a murderer.

Counsel. That remains to be seen, Russell. But you have threatened to murder, haven't you?

Russell. No. I've never ...

Counsel. Come, Russell! You've threatened to kill. And on more than one occasion.

Russell. No. I can't remember ever having ...

Counsel. Are your threats to kill so off-handed? So inconsequential? So easily forgotten?

Russell. I'm sorry. I don't know what you're talking about.

Counsel. Do you remember a project called Summerfield Court?

Russell. Yes. It was ...

Counsel. A block of luxury flats, built by your firm, I think?

Russell. Yes.

Counsel. We're talking about a time, before you retired from active work?

Russell. Yes. Ten years ago ... about.

Counsel. Eleven, to be precise.

Russell. If you say so.

Counsel. Before your partnership with Sir William Macks.

Russell. I was a working bricklayer, if that's what you mean.

Counsel. I'm obliged, Russell. That's exactly what I mean. Now—the Summerfield Court project—you had a dual responsibility, had you not?

Russell. I don't understand.

Counsel. You were responsible for the completion of those flats?

Russell. There was a lot of sub-contracting.

Counsel. But the overall responsibility was still yours, surely?

Russell. Yes. I'd taken the job on.

Counsel. And, in addition to that, you had the normal responsibility of a skilled workman, on a site?

Russell. Yes. I suppose so.

Counsel. A dual responsibility, in fact?

Russell. Yes. I suppose I had.

Counsel. The Summerfield Court project. A large job?

Russell. Yes.

Counsel. For a firm of your size—of your size, at that time, I mean—how large?

Russell. Very large. At that time, the biggest thing we'd ever done.

Counsel. Specifically, how large?

Russell. A quarter of a million. Just over a quarter of a million.

Counsel. Pounds?

Russell. Yes, pounds.

Counsel. You obtained the contract, against what sort of opposition?

Russell. Other tenders were submitted.

Counsel. Of course. Go on, please.

Russell. Ours wasn't the cheapest. We had a policy. You paid for the best, and you got the best. We still work on that principle.

Counsel. An admirable principle, Russell. Now, about the electrical work, on the Summerfield Court flats?

Russell. It was sub-contracted.

Counsel. Ah, yes. Now, I would draw your mind to a certain electrician. To the installation of certain wall-lights.

Russell. I don't remember the details. If you have a copy of the plans ...

Counsel. No. The plans are unnecessary, Russell. I wish to remind you of an incident. Of an electrician who cut a run for wires, to a proposed wall-light. He cut this run along a newly-plastered wall. Do you remember the incident, Russell?

Russell. Yes. I—I think so.

Counsel. You aren't sure?

Russell. It's a long time ago.

Counsel. I could call witnesses. To jog your memory. If that's what you prefer.

Russell. No. I remember.

Counsel. Well?

Russell. Yes ... well.

Counsel. How well?

Russell. Look, I don't know what ...

Counsel. Demonstrate to the court, how well you remember the incident, Russell. Tell the court what happened.

Russell. I threw a brick at him.

Counsel. At the electrician?

Russell. Yes.

Counsel. From what distance?

Russell. I don't know. I forget.

Counsel. A room-length?

Russell. No. Less than that.

Counsel. Two yards? Three yards?

Russell. Yes. About three yards.

Counsel. Did you throw the brick hard?

Russell. Yes ... I threw it hard.

Counsel. As hard as you were able?

Russell. Yes.

Counsel. Did it hit the electrician?

Russell. Yes.

Counsel. Where?

Russell. In the face.

Counsel. Please speak up, Russell. The court wishes to hear your answers. Where did the brick hit the unfortunate electrician?

Russell. In the face. It hit him in the face.

Counsel. Did it cause injury?

Russell. Yes.

Counsel. To what degree?

Russell. He was away from work for a few weeks.

Counsel. A few weeks?

Russell. About two months. Just over two months. He didn't come back to the Summerfield Court site.

Counsel. Hospital treatment?

Russell. Yes. He was in hospital, for a while.

Counsel. There was some possibility that he might lose the sight of one eye ... is my information correct?

Russell. There was talk. But he didn't.

Counsel. Nevertheless, he did suffer severe facial injuries?

Russell. Yes.

Counsel. Right—now, having thrown the brick at this man—what did you attempt to do next?

Russell. I don't know what you mean.

Counsel. Having thrown the brick at the man, what was your next move?

Russell. Oh!

Counsel. Yes?

Russell. I—er—I went for him with a brick-hammer.

Counsel. Attacked him?

Russell. Yes.

Counsel. With a brick-hammer?

Russell. Yes. But the men held me off. I didn't ...

Counsel. Supposing the men hadn't been there, Russell?

Russell. What?

Counsel. Supposing the men hadn't 'held you off'. What would have happened? What would have been the outcome?

Russell. Well ... I—er ...

Counsel. Would you have inflicted even more injuries upon this wretched electrician? More injuries? This time with a brick-hammer?

Russell. Yes. I suppose so.

Counsel. Quite. I, too, 'suppose so'. I have little doubt the court, also, 'supposes so'.

Russell. Look! I know it sounds as if ...

Counsel. This man—this electrician—he is in need of urgent hospital treatment. There is a possibility that he will lose the sight of one eye. He is severely injured, about the face. Why, Russell? Why?

Russell. Well ... Because the brick hit him in the face, and, ...

Counsel. No. I mean why throw the brick? Why throw the brick, in the first place?

Russell. He'd—he'd made an unholy mess of the wall.

Counsel. How?

Russell. It had just been plastered, and he ruined it.

Counsel. By cutting a path, for his wire, into the plaster and down to the brickwork?

Russell. Yes.

Counsel. Just that one wall?

Russell. Yes. Just that one wall.

Counsel. All the wall?

Russell. What?

Counsel. Did the whole wall have to be re-plastered?

Russell. No. Not all of it. But part of it had to be faced up and skimmed off.

Counsel. Right. Now, for the benefit of the court, Russell, let me see if I've got my facts right. We're talking about a project, contracted out to your firm, for a quarter of a million pounds?

Russell. Just over a quarter of a million.

Counsel. And this was not—to use an expression—a 'tight contract'?

Russell. We don't undercut.

Counsel. Quite. In other words, your clients were getting the best, but they were paying for the best.

Russell. I've already said. We've always worked on that principle.

Counsel. Which, in turn, means a good margin of profit?

Russell. Not outrageous. Moderate.

Counsel. But sufficient?

Russell. We priced it out. We allowed for a moderate profit.

Counsel. Quite. But, a 'moderate profit', on a quarter-of-a-million-pound project represents a considerable sum ... surely?

Russell. The bigger the job, the bigger the profit. But that doesn't mean ...

Counsel. A considerable sum, Russell. Certainly a sum, by comparison with which, the cost of re-plastering a wall—even supposing a whole wall needs re-plastering—is negligible.

Russell. I—I suppose so.

Counsel. I beg your pardon, Russell. I didn't quite catch that answer.

Russell. Yes. Looked at it that way. I suppose so.

Counsel. What might almost come under the heading of

a 'minor miscalculation'? Something for which due allowance was made, in the tender?

Russell. Yes. All right ... yes.

Counsel. Why throw the brick, Russell?

Russell. I lost my temper.

Counsel. At such a little thing?

Russell. It wasn't a ...

Counsel. At such an understandable mistake? At an error —an error so small that, when it is compared with the surrounding circumstances, it becomes almost laughable—and, for this unimportant error, you deliberately caused grievous injury to an innocent man? And your only excuse is that you lost your temper?

Russell. Put that way, it sounds bad.

Counsel. Those were the circumstances, surely?

Russell. Yes ... put that way.

Counsel. That you lost control of your temper?

Russell. Yes ... I suppose so.

Counsel. Unreasonably? And without cause?

Russell. Put that way ...

Counsel. Is there a better way of putting it?

Russell. No. Probably not.

Counsel. A more truthful way?

Russell. No. I don't suppose so.

Counsel. And do you still tell this court that you are not a man given to extreme violence?

Russell. I do.

Counsel. That you do not have an uncontrollable temper?

Russell. No. I don't have an uncontrollable temper.

Counsel. I can find no reference to your having been prosecuted for this attack—this vicious and unprovoked attack—upon this electrician.

Russell. No. I wasn't.

Counsel. I beg your pardon?

Russell. I wasn't prosecuted. It—er—didn't reach the police.

Counsel. Are you telling the court that this matter was never reported to the police?

Russell. It was ...

Counsel. Yes?

Russell. Settled out of court. We agreed not to ...

Counsel. That's impossible, Russell.

Russell. That's what we ...

Counsel. You can't 'settle' a criminal assault 'out of court', Russell. Not an assault of that magnitude. What you did, of course, was bribe the unfortunate electrician into silence. Am I right?

Russell. We—er—paid him what he asked. No quibbling.

Counsel. Bribery, nevertheless.

Russell. I suppose ... It could be called that. We didn't want bad publicity.

Counsel. Bearing in mind the incident at the Summerfield Court project—bearing that in mind—when the character witnesses we have heard describe you as a 'reasonable man', and even a 'kindly man', do you not think they're mistaken?

Russell. No. I don't think they're mistaken. I think they're honest.

Counsel. Oh, I don't doubt their honesty, Russell. I don't doubt their sincerity. But I doubt the basis of their belief. And I wonder whether the electrician, who still carries facial scars, would share their belief.

CHAPTER SIX

The Stag stretches its metal bonnet out, towards Colbank. And, beyond Colbank, towards the city and Alderman Roebuck. The tyres whisper their road-noise along the tarmac. And whisper, and whisper, like conspirators planning some gigantic, and never-ending, evil. Night creeps nearer, via that dusky half-light, which is neither darkness nor light. It is the yawn of the day; before day finally retires and night blinks wide its electric eyes, and takes control.

And I remember that character assassination.

The barrister who prosecuted did his job, as well as he was able ... and his job was to prosecute. But facts, without explanations—facts, without cause—don't add up to the truth. They're like cheap wood, stained and grained to resemble walnut. Like pebble-dashing, covering poor brickwork.

And a courtroom is not a building site.

That electrician's job was to get the wiring into position, before the plasterer even started. There is a way of doing these things. A sequence. And that sequence is one of the many differences between skilled work, and unskilled work.

The plasterer was my man. He'd done a good job. That wall was a single entity—a single, uninterrupted area of craftsmanship—and that electrician had ruined its perfection.

Like flawing a precious stone.

Like daubing a good painting.

And, although it was re-plastered, and re-skimmed, it had a fault, and that nobody could *see* the fault didn't alter the fact. *I* knew it had a fault ... and that was enough.

It wasn't the money. It wasn't the piffling cost of re-plastering the wall. It was the *principle*. It was the realisation that here was a man who claimed to be a fully-qualified craftsman, and who was being paid the wage of a fully-qualified craftsman, and who'd been let loose on something for which *I* was responsible, and who hadn't cared. Who hadn't given a damn about what was beneath the surface. Who hadn't given a damn about the *inside* quality.

I know why I threw that brick.

I know that, in similar circumstances, I'd throw another brick ... and, these days, even harder!

And why not?

Pride. A reputation. Utter reliability. These qualities—a reputation for these qualities—don't come easily. They don't come cheaply. They have to be worked for, fought for and paid for. And, when you have them, it needs even more work, more fight and more pay to hang onto them.

Something that prosecuting barrister didn't mention.

Something he probably wouldn't know about.

CHAPTER SEVEN

I am getting a little drunk.

I drain the last of the whisky from my glass and, almost from a distance, notice that my hand has a slight tremble. I push back my chair, stand up from the table and walk, carefully, towards the bar-counter.

I have never visited this hotel before, but I have stayed in scores of its sister-hotels. It is of a kind, and there are too many of that kind. Its musty finery has all the gaiety of a plush shroud. Its waiters have the droll solemnity of morticians, and their grey-white jackets carry the sparkling look of mourning.

This place, and its kind, personifies the undead.

And, why not? The people who stay in such places—who even drink in such places—are dead, anyway. Their eyes are without life. Their expressions are without animation. They sit in the lounge bar, and perform the ritualistic farce of pouring liquor down their throats, sip at a time. One, two—never more than three—at a table. Silent and morose, or whisper-talking, like grave-robbing ghouls. The well-dressed and the affluent zombies, enjoying their Thursday night drinking session.

I reach the bar.

I say, 'One double-whisky, with its own weight in water. And ice.'

The young man behind the bar moves his head. He seems surprised to find one more living creature in this corner of the world.

The booze has sharpened my irritation.

'You *are* here to take orders?' I ask, sarcastically.

'Eh?'

'Or are you rehearsing the role of second grave-digger?'

'Sorry?' He allows a slow, shamefaced grin to reach his mouth. 'What is it you wanted, sir?'

I repeat the order.

I pay him, and say, 'This place. What happens on Thursday night?'

'Not a lot,' he says, honestly. 'Thursdays—Fridays—Saturdays—any day of the week. In this place, not a lot happens.'

I grunt my disgust.

He says, 'The cinema. There's two.'

'Really?'

'*The Sound of Music. The Nympho.*'

'Good God!'

He grins, and says, 'With luck, they'll get the reels mixed. That should be good for a laugh.'

I replace my scowl with a watered-down smile.

'Or,' he says, 'there's the local amateur operatic society. They should start murdering *The Maid of the Mountains* within the hour. Knowing the leading tenor, he'll probably rape her, first.'

43

I drain some of the water from my smile. After my initial reaction, I am beginning to like this young bar-keeper's dry sense of humour.

I say, 'Join me. Let's make it a double-bedded morgue.'

'Thanks. Lager okay?'

'Lager it is.'

I hand back the requisite cash. He pours a lager, tastes it and smacks his lips, appreciatively.

In a low voice, he says, 'If it's talent you're after ...'

I curl my hand around the whisky, and mock him gently with my eyes.

He talks without moving his lips. Without taking his gaze from a corner of the ceiling.

He murmurs, 'I could fix it. Not too expensive. No questions, and nothing compromising. Here—in one of the bedrooms ... if that's what you want.'

'Does the manager know?' I ask, softly.

'If he does, he doesn't care.'

'That must be very convenient.'

'Nothing too startling, I'm afraid. Nothing very avant-garde.'

My gentle chuckle isn't loud enough to reach his ears.

He continued, 'They don't go in for *The Perfumed Garden* bit, in these parts.'

'And randy with it,' I say, quietly.

He lowers his eyes, and looks at me, questioningly.

'Nice try, youth,' I smile. 'You've done your best. But I'm getting a bit ancient.'

'If you knew some of the old goats who sniff around, after ...'

'Sorry. Not this old goat.' I raise my glass and, as the whisky is en route to my lips, I have a brainwave. I say, 'Roebuck. D'you know him?'

'Roebuck?'

'Alderman Roebuck,' I amplify.

'Er ...'

44

I drink, swallow, then say, 'Of The Garth.'

'Of—er—of The Garth?'

As I lower my glass, I say, 'D'you know him?'

He tastes the lager, and watches me carefully.

Then, he says, 'You're a friend of his?'

I shake my head.

'A business acquaintance? Something like that?'

'No. Not an acquaintance.'

'But, somebody you know?' he angles.

'I know the name. That's all.'

I slip my wallet from its pocket, peel a five pound note from its slot, and drop the money onto the bar counter.

I say, 'Take a risk, youth. Earn yourself the price of a short time with some of the talent you've just been trying to sell me. Alderman Maurice Roebuck. Tell me about him.'

He plugs what he thinks is the last rat-hole.

He says, 'You a copper?'

I almost laugh in his face.

He says, 'No-o—okay ... you're not the law. What is it you want to know?'

I wait until he has pocketed the five pound note.

Then, I say, 'Let's start with the basic question. Would you let your daughter marry Maurice Roebuck?'

'Eh?' He stares.

'That's what I want,' I explain. 'What his morals are. What makes him tick. What keeps him alive, and interested.'

'Money,' comes the short, snappy answer.

'So easy?'

'With Roebuck—yeah ... so easy.'

I raise questioning eyebrows.

The bar-keeper says, 'He's a fixer. There's one on every council. He's ours.'

'Good?' I ask.

'As good as the money makes him. Big, and small. You

45

want a "Cycling Prohibited" notice slapped across the path, behind your house. He's the man to contact. It'll go up.'

'For a price?'

'Naturally ... for a small consideration.'

'Naturally,' I murmur.

'He's also a J.P.'

'Uhu?'

'It helps if you're snapped up on a motoring charge.'

'Bent?' I ask, mildly.

As I ask the question I raise my glass, and watch the youth's face from above the rim.

He moves his shoulders, and says, 'Depends what you call bent.'

'Unstraight,' I amplify.

'Most of 'em are ... aren't they?'

'You,' I warn, 'are in grave danger of growing into a cynic.'

'Most of 'em *are*,' he insists. 'I've heard 'em horse-trading in this place, too many times.'

'Roebuck?'

'More than once,' he assures me.

The lager and the whisky help the silence along for a few minutes.

The youth moves down the bar to replenish the glass of an elderly man who looks as if he is on vacation from the local cemetery, then returns and finishes the lager in one, moderately long, swallow.

He lowers the glass, then says, 'I can tell you where he'll be.'

'Roebuck?'

'If you're interested.'

'Roebuck interests me,' I admit.

He gives me a lewd wink, then says, 'There's a glorified knocking-shop.'

'You're the right age,' I observe, drily.

46

'Eh?'

'You have a one-track mind.'

'Of course.'

'One-track ... straight to some woman's thighs.'

'Yeah ... but what a lovely journey.' He grins.

'Roebuck.' I nudge him back onto the subject-matter.

'That's where he'll be.'

'In a brothel?'

'We-ell ...'

'In *this* town?'

I have doubts, and the doubts hang themselves on my question.

'Not a brothel,' he protests, softly. 'Not a *brothel*.'

'That's what you said.'

'It's not supposed to be.' He moves his hands in tiny, palm-upward gestures. 'It's a club—y'know ... a club. Very respectable.'

'It sounds it.'

'Y'know ... art, for art's sake. That sort of thing.'

'What sort of a club?'

'A cine club.'

I tilt my head, suspiciously, and say, 'Blue movies? Is that what you're telling me?'

'Members, and guests.'

'And?'

'Thursday night ... "Continental Night". They have some rooms, off the auditorium. Y'know ... where members can "discuss".'

' "Discuss"?'

'The merits of the films.'

'With—er—"guests"?'

He smiles, knowingly.

I say, 'Let's assume you're not being over-imaginative. Let's assume Thursday night is "Continental Night", and Roebuck is sitting there, enjoying a cinematograph orgy. How does that help?'

47

'I'm a member.'

'You *would* be.'

'I'm not stuck behind this bar *every* Thursday.' He pats the pocket into which he has slipped the five pound note. "This buys you the loan of my membership card.'

I feel a warning tingle, at the nape of my neck.

This youth has a keen mind. Possibly a little *too* keen ... and I am in no hurry to feel its cutting edge across my throat.

I move cautiously.

I say, 'Steady the Buffs, youth. You're taking too much for granted.'

'You wanted to see Alderman Roebuck.'

'Oh, no.' I shake my head. 'I asked about him. You're the one who pinpointed his whereabouts. I didn't ask *that.*'

'True.' He makes the admission with over-emphasised ponderousness. He furrows his forehead, stares, out-of-focus, across the room, and muses, 'You didn't ask *where* he was.'

'That, I did not.'

'Only *what* he was.'

'Correct.'

'And, I haven't asked who *you* are. Or *what* you are.'

'Don't waste good questions,' I murmur.

'So-o—strictly speaking—you've bought me a drink, and given me a king-sized tip, for sweet F.A. That doesn't happen very often. When it does, I'm appreciative.'

He turns his back, and ducks into an alcove at the rear of the bar. When he returns, he says, 'Excuse me, sir. I have other customers waiting to be served.'

He moves off, down the bar.

There are no other customers waiting to be served. I am the only person at the bar-counter and, for something to do, he polishes glasses which are already clean.

On the counter, in front of me, he has left a triangle of folded cardboard, with a mock-leather binding. The

48

words 'Membership Card' are in gold, against the green. It is there for the taking ... and no questions asked, or answered.

So, why not?

I slip the card into my pocket, as I finish the whisky.

CHAPTER EIGHT

I could have taken a taxi. Or, I could have taken the Stag, from the park of the hotel, and driven around, looking for Manston Hall in comfort.

I decided against the Stag because, being lost in a strange town, in a motor car, is *really* being lost. Driving around unknown streets—usually badly lit streets—steering a car, watching for traffic signs, searching for street names, and then for a specific building, once you've found the street, is not the most tranquil way of spending an evening.

I decided against the Stag.

Nevertheless, I *could* have taken a taxi.

I didn't ... for two reasons.

Cab drivers have notoriously good memories; the better firms even log the various journeys. What I was going to say to Roebuck—supposing I even *found* Roebuck—was something I hadn't given much thought to ... or, come to that, have yet given much thought to.

I know Roebuck only as a scoundrel. As a man who has creamed a personal, ten-thousand-pound nest-egg, from one of the best, and one of the most complex, projects the firm has ever tendered for, and won. As a man who has performed this abomination behind my back, and in such a manner that, if the involved knot of figures, deals and counter-deals is ever satisfactorily untangled, the resulting

49

exposure *must* ruin the reputation of R. & M.

I know him as the purchaser of the Toledo; the Toledo he'd either given, or sold, to Lissa; the Toledo which was parked outside Yew Cottage on the night of the murder.

I don't know Roebuck, but, when I left the hotel, I hoped to *get* to know him.

Therefore, no cab driver.

My second reason for not using a taxi was, because I felt like some air.

I am now getting some of that air.

Good old north country air. Mixed with good old north country soot. Mixed with good old north country muck. And, for good measure, mixed with good old north country rain.

Rain, in these parts, is a form of liquid misery. The skies weep, as if in memory of a green and pleasant land, buried in a graveyard of mills and railway sidings—slag-heaps and canal basins—factories and brick-works. The north. The grit and guts of the north. The one place on earth where the Industrial Revolution still steamrollers men into broken shells.

And where—or so it seems—there are at least half a dozen Manston Halls.

I have already asked five people. I have been pointed north, south, east and west. I have been given street directions guaranteed to baffle a cross-eyed Chinaman but, at last, I have found the place.

Apart from the crumbling portal-work, it could be a warehouse. It has the dimensions, and the shape, of a small warehouse. Angular, red-brick and unimaginative. Its entrance is up an alley, from a side street which, in turn, leads from one of the better-lit roads. The glow from the yellow street-lighting of the road gives dim illumination to the side street, but leaves the alley in darkness, except for a slight overspill from a couple of lighted windows in the building itself.

I turn into the alley, and a voice says, 'Russell.'
It is a man's voice. Soft, and slightly questioning.
I stop, half-turn, and say, 'Yes. Who is ...'
And real darkness arrives. With a rush.
Odd ... but I don't feel a thing.

CHAPTER NINE

I can certainly feel things *now*.

The old dear in the plastic mac and rain-bonnet is tut-tutting and now-then-luving all over me. She is a nice person. She is doing her best, and I have no wish to throw up all over her pouter bosom. But, unless I feel much better, soon, that is exactly what I am going to do.

The back of my skull feels as if the Concorde has crash-landed on my hair-line. The beam from a torch is par-boiling my out-of-focus eyes. My clothes are soaked and filthy. And half the population of this rotten town are standing, chattering, gawping down at me and dripping rain-water from their hats and umbrellas.

I choke back my stomach-contents, and raise my fingers to the back of my head.

I mumble, 'Wha ... What the hell ...'

'You fell, luv,' volunteers the old dear in the plastic mac. 'I reckon you musta slipped, on the wet cobbles.'

Somebody says, 'It's orright, mister. She's a nurse. She knows wot she's doing.'

'I'm a nurse, luv,' echoes the old dear.

Another voice says, 'We've sent for an ambulance.'

'It's on its way, luv.' The old dear tightens her arms around my shoulders. It won't be long, now.'

'No,' I mutter. 'No ambulance.'

I look at my fingers. They are stained with watered-down blood. I try to push myself from the ground, and the world starts spinning a little.

The old dear says, 'Easy, luv. Take it easy.'

I force the merry-go-round to a slow halt then, very shakily, heave myself upright. I find a convenient wall, and lean against it. They all stare at me, as if I am Lazarus doing his recovery trick. The fool with the torch still fancies himself as a spotlight operator, and doesn't help.

The old dear says, 'Look, luv, take it easy for a few minutes.' She sounds genuinely worried. 'There's an ambulance on its way.'

'No ambulance,' I croak. 'Thanks for the thought ... but no ambulance.'

The ambulance, with a squad car escort, arrives at the scene.

For the next fifty years, or so, there is a multi-voiced argument. It concerns itself with the state of my health, my possible identity and the use (or non-use) of an ambulance. Everybody contributes an unasked for opinion. The police toss questions, but get no answers. The ambulance men are eager to perform their stretcher-and-blankets routine. The old dear is almost in tears, because I refuse her a Florence Nightingale trip. Everybody mills around, making noise and tripping over each other's feet.

The show continues, non-stop, for about fifty years.

Then, I take a couple of deep breaths, and push myself away from the wall.

I snarl, 'Piss off. The lot of you ... *piss off!*'

They part, and allow me to walk, unsteadily, from where I have been clobbered. One of the squad men makes a token attempt at stepping into my line of walk, but I glare at him, and he moves aside.

Me?

I want the hotel. I want the use of a bathroom. I want

the use of a sponge, and some cleaning fluid, for my clothes.

After that, there is a certain young bar-keeper, whose teeth I am anxious to extract ... the hard way!

CHAPTER TEN

It is one hour into a new day. Friday. The rain is coming down, as if this year is St Swithin's benefit year. I have bathed, re-dressed, stoked myself back into near-normality with a couple of brandies, and am now leaning with my thumb on a bell-push. The rectangle of card, above the bell-push, reads W. Williamson and, if the night porter at the hotel is to be believed, W. Williamson is the name of a smooth-talking young pup who handed me a certain Membership Card. The said W. Williamson apparently lives out his miserable existence in one of these jerry-converted, self-contained flats in this Victorian monstrosity of a house. There is a deep porch over the entrance and, apart from shielding me from the rain, this porch provides a degree of secrecy, supposing W. Williamson wishes to check the identity of his small-hours visitor, before answering the bell.

And he *will* answer. He will answer, because my thumb stays on this button until the door opens.

He answers.

The latch-lock is turned, the door is opened, and there he stands, in all his virile magnificence. Bog-eyed from disturbed sleep. Tousle-haired. Wearing a Marks and Sparks shortie dressing-gown, over striped pyjamas. Bare-footed and dirty-nailed.

He looks like an animated ad. for the morning after.

He blinks, and says, 'Whaaa ...'

I take my thumb from the bell-push, grab two handfuls of dressing-gown, plant the sole of one shoe against the jamb and do a push-pull action ... with every ounce of strength I can muster.

He leaves the doorway like a cork leaving a shaken champagne-bottle. He doesn't even touch the four shallow steps leading up to the door. As he sprawls on the tarmac drive he gives a high yelp of pain, and grabs a shoulder. I think his collar bone has snapped ... and the thought does a lot towards making me feel warm and happy.

I follow him down the steps, hoick him into a more, or less, upright position and slap him across the face a few times.

I say, 'This is the scenario for your next home-movie, youth. Get Roebuck to add the camera-angles. And, next time, tell him to make a better casting job ... never ask a man who's been charged with murder to play the part of the patsy.'

I end with a full-blooded punch in the mouth, and he rockets backwards before spreadeagling himself in the sodden soil of a badly-tended rose bed where, as a small bonus, the thorns cause him additional discomfort.

I walk away from the house, and back towards the parked Stag.

The back of my head still throbs a little ... but I now have the comfort of knowing it is not the only hurt in the world.

CHAPTER ELEVEN

I find the nearest motorway, and spend the few hours left, before dawn, in an all-night, service-area café. I settle into a corner bench, drink tea, smoke cigarettes, then try to sleep a little.

I dream, but I do not dream. Like a swimmer, floating on the surface of water, I float on the surface of sleep and, like the undulations of tiny waves, half-dreams, which are distorted memories, touch me, stir me and refuse me complete slumber.

I am back in the morgue and, once more, Crawford glances at me, before folding back the sheet to expose the thing which is on the slab. The dead thing, with the burned and tortured face; with the horrific head, and the hair which has been burned from the scalp, and the blackened tissue, where the cheeks and neck should be.

'We need formal identification ... if possible,' says Crawford, gently.

I nod. I can't trust myself to speak.

Crawford says, 'I'm sorry, Russell. But, if possible, we have to be *absolutely* sure.'

Again, I nod.

I stare down at the face which is no longer a face.

Crawford says, 'We're pretty sure it's her. Jewellery. Contents of the handbag, The car. Even fingerprints ... we've managed a couple, and tied them in with prints in the car. But—coroners ... wherever possible, they need official confirmation from next-of-kin.'

For a third time, I nod dumb understanding.

I take the sheet from his fingers and, gradually, unveil

this dead thing a little further. Until the hands are exposed. I take one of the hands in mine—the right hand —and turn it, to look at the palm.

The hand is cold. Cold! Colder than anything I have touched in my life, before. Cold, and dead, but not stiff. I expected it to be stiff, but it is limp ... and *cold*.

It is burned. The back of the hand and the fingers are burned ... but part of the palm has been saved from the flames. And, on Lissa's palm there is a scar. Such a tiny scar. A scar she has carried for years. A scar from a slipped can-opener.

I look at the palm.

I return the hand to the side of this dead thing.

I cover the burned and tortured flesh with the clean, white sheet.

'Well?' asks Crawford, gently.

I say, 'It's her. It's my wife ... Lissa.'

And Lissa, and what was once Lissa, and the distorted memory of Lissa float with me, on the surface of sleep, and deny me rest.

CHAPTER TWELVE

R. v. RUSSELL.
Extract from Record of Trial.
Cross-examination of Accused, by Prosecuting Counsel.
Counsel. Russell, you have told this court that, when you arrived at the cottage known as Yew Cottage, you found the cottage already burning.
Russell. Yes.
Counsel. Blazing?
Russell. I'm sorry. I don't ...

Counsel. Was it blazing? For example, were flames coming from the windows? From the roof, perhaps?

Russell. No. There was a flickering light, from inside. As if something was on fire.

Counsel. From inside the building?

Russell. Yes.

Counsel. A flickering light?

Russell. Yes.

Counsel. And then, as I understand your evidence, you smashed a window, in order to gain entry?

Russell. Yes.

Counsel. The cottage was your home, was it not?

Russell. It was where I lived, most of the time.

Counsel. Your home?

Russell. Yes.

Counsel. You'd have a key, presumably?

Russell. Well—yes—but ...

Counsel. Why didn't you use the key, Russell? Why didn't you enter in a normal way? Why break a window?

Russell. I don't know. It's hard to say. I think I must have panicked.

Counsel. Do you panic easily, Russell?

Russell. No. I don't think so.

Counsel. Then, why this time? Why panic at this time? The fire wasn't excessive. There were no flames coming from the cottage. Just a flickering light. So, what made you panic?

Russell. I—I don't know.

Counsel. You—er—don't know?

Russell. No. I don't know.

Counsel. Because you miscalculated, perhaps?

Russell. I'm sorry. I don't know what ...

Counsel. Having murdered your wife. Having set fire ...

Russell. I did not murder my wife.

Counsel. Having set fire to the body, and the cottage, you miscalculated the spread of the fire.

Russell. That's not true.

Counsel. You left the cottage, by the door, of course. You left it burning.

Russell. No.

Counsel. Intending to return. Intending to apparently 'find' the cottage in flames. And all evidence of your wife's murder destroyed.

Russell. That is not true.

Counsel. But you miscalculated. You returned too soon. The fire had spread more slowly than you'd calculated. The evidence wasn't destroyed. And you panicked.

Russell. I didn't kill my wife. I didn't set fire to Yew Cottage. And I didn't panic.

Counsel. You didn't panic?

Russell. No. I did not panic.

Counsel. Forgive me, Russell, but that isn't what you said a moment ago. I asked you, if you remember, why you broke a window, to gain entry? Why you didn't use the door? Your answer was, 'I think I must have panicked'. Did you panic?

Russell. No. Not the way you mean.

Counsel. The way I mean?

Russell. I didn't panic because I was guilty. Because I'd murdered my wife.

Counsel. Did you panic, Russell?

Russell. Yes. A little. Because the cottage was on fire. Because I didn't know what was happening.

Counsel. You panicked?

Russell. Yes. I've already said. Because ...

Counsel. You—a man who, on your own evidence, does not panic easily—suddenly panicked. Why, Russell? Why suddenly panic in this mysterious way?

CHAPTER THIRTEEN

Lissa. *Lissa! LISSA!*

We had everything. I had pride; pride in myself, and pride in my craft.

You had beauty; beauty which was more than skin-deep, and beauty which was not from a cosmetic jar.

We had just about everything going for us.

But pride corrupts—and beauty corrupts—and we were both ridiculously corruptible, and there was a change. There was a hidden flaw, somewhere. There was a canker.

We argued. Then we fought. Then we were incapable of normal man-and-wife conversation; a single word, and we were back to fighting each other again.

We made up. Then we didn't make up. Then the thought of even *trying* to make up never even entered our minds.

I grew blind, and didn't see your beauty ... I only heard your bickering.

You also grew blind, and didn't see my pride ... you only saw my pig-headedness.

Then, gradually—and, at the end, with a rush—what little love we had left soured and blackened into an evil emotion. But not hatred. Never *hatred*! Disgust, perhaps ... but never quite hatred.

We both demanded perfection from the other, and neither of us was perfect.

And now, you're dead. And buried. And forgotten.

God!

If only you *were* ... if only you *were* forgotten.

Lissa, my lovely, I have learned a great and wonderful

philosophy; a great and wonderful truth. Nobody dies. *Nobody*. While ever some person who knew them lives— and while ever some person who knew *that* person lives— death is a fallacy. We all live, forever. Everybody! While ever a name is remembered, and while ever somebody speaks that name, the owner of the name lives on.

Immortality.

'You're immortal, Lissa.'

You're dead ... but you'll live throughout my forever.

CHAPTER FOURTEEN

The edge of sleep. The shore-line, between consciousness and unconsciousness, with all the washed-up debris of truths, and half-truths, would-be-truths, and wishful truths, dreams and nightmares.

When your mental feet are bogged down in the soft sand of utter weariness, and you're too tired to stagger back into the real world, and too frightened to paddle out into the Waters of Nod.

Judas Christ ... what a night!

CHAPTER FIFTEEN

The motorway, like every other motorway, slices its way through some magnificent countryside, but dawn in the countryside can be just as miserable as dawn in any city. It can be just as damp, just as grey, and just as wretched.

Take now ...

My mouth is in need of a de-coke, my eyes feel as if they've been sand-blasted and, although this service-area café is surrounded by landscape about which either Turner or Constable might have raved, it is still dawn, it is still wet and misty and it is still miserable.

I stare out of the window, at the dripping, leafless branches; at the patches of brown, dead grass in a meadow; at a family of poverty-stricken bluetits practising gymnastics along the edge of the café roof.

It is still March, and March is a lousy month, the world over.

I find the men's room, splash my face with cold water, dry myself on the usual starched-stiff roller-towel, then return to the café for a breakfast of baked beans on toast.

I smoke my first cigarette of the day and, as I smoke, an urge builds up inside me. A desire takes shape; a desire to know exactly *what*.

Some answers I already have. Others, I can guess. But there are still questions, without answers attached ... and those questions concern a death.

And, with this growing desire for the complete truth, comes a realisation. That Crawford was speaking no less than the truth, when he first saw me in the cell area, yesterday; that I *was* suffering from a form of delayed shock ... and that the shock is only now wearing off.

It started with the arrest, and the never-ending interrogations. It continued with the de-humanising routine of the prison. It culminated with the trial, and the (to me) unexpected verdict. For weeks, I have been numb. For weeks, I have allowed self-pity to choke me. For weeks, I have been manipulated. Manipulated! Without fighting back. Without resisting. Without doing *anything* ... like a moth, caught in a killing-bottle.

I sip luke-warm tea. I smoke this first, Friday cigarette.

And the fury rises, like a tide and, for the first time for weeks, I am capable of true rage.

I am, once more, myself.

I am, once more, the real and complete Harvey Russell.

CHAPTER SIXTEEN

Where else, but a detective agency?

Like most things, they come in all sizes. The back-street, key-hole peepers who collect divorce dirt. The firms who earn insurance-company retainers; whose job it is to ferret out swindlers and bankruptcy bandits. Those are the two ends of a wide spectrum, and the colours between range from near-black to soiled white. None are *quite* pure; even the best are capable of bending the spirit of the law, until it screams with agony, if the client is important enough ... which means, if his pocket is deep enough.

I have a very deep pocket ... and I want action!

Like this one, the top agencies usually have an ex-cop at their head, and a good percentage of their work force are also ex-fuzz.

I have used this one a couple of times, before. When rabble-rousers have threatened to disrupt the smooth working of a big site; to gather enough dirt to put on the black, and give hard warning to some anarchistic bastard who was dreaming up nightmares for R. & M.

It is a good firm. A tough firm; a firm not given to pussyfooting around if, and when, decisions need taking. Its head man is Kelly—Charles Kelly, ex-chief superintendent of police—and Charlie Kelly is a copper of the old school, which means he is an iron man, and stands in second place to nobody.

We sit in his roomy office, and I tell him what I want, and he listens.

Then he asks questions.

'Crawford?' he says. 'D'you know him?'

'Not socially.'

'No ... but professionally?'

'The murder.'

'He interviewed you?'

I agree that Crawford interviewed me.

'Hard?'

I agree that Crawford's interviews deserve the description of 'hard'.

'Often?'

I agree that the interviews were 'often'.

'How often?' asks Kelly.

'He asked a whale of a lot of questions,' I growl.

'Before he charged you? After he charged you?'

'Before, *and* after.'

'I'm puzzled,' muses Kelly. 'What the hell made you make that admission?'

I know the answer to that one, too, but it is difficult to explain. It is almost impossible to explain to a man like Kelly.

The admission was false, but necessary. Necessary, because I was still dazed as a result of the investigation, the arrest, the remand in prison and the trial. I came out of that dock, like a sleep-walker; every ounce of resistance had been sapped out of me and, although I didn't know it at the time, I was scared stupid. At that moment, I wanted friendship, like a drowning man wants a lifeline. I wanted something—somebody—to grab, and hold, in order to prevent myself from slipping over the edge.

Crawford offered me that for which I craved, and I was in his debt. I took what he offered. Gladly. Eagerly. I pay my debts, and I owed him something. I gave him what I thought he most wanted.

63

I try to explain all this to Kelly. I hope he understands ... that, yesterday, I was a psychiatrist's dream boy.

'Brain-washing,' grunts Kelly.

'I—er—I suppose so.'

I haven't viewed it from that angle, before.

Kelly says, 'You don't need truth drugs. Any good copper can do it.'

'Crawford's a good copper.'

'*Can* ... but *doesn't*.'

'Oh!'

'I can name half a dozen men,' says Kelly, sourly. 'Given time, they'd all admit to the murder of Martin Luther King. *And* plead Guilty.'

'That's a powerful remark,' I muse.

'Mind over mind ... it's a powerful weapon, Russell. You've just had a taste of it. You should know.'

He opens a desk drawer, takes out smoking equipment and goes through the rigmarole peculiar to pipe-smokers. The pipe is a leather-covered, Italian job; the cheaper ones are passed across a counter, in exchange for a five pound note ... and this is not a cheap one. The pig-skin pouch goes with the pipe. I have no doubt the tobacco does not put its holder to shame. Kelly retired as a police chief superintendent ... but, today, he probably pays triple his pension in income tax.

He fiddles with the pipe and tobacco, asks questions and makes observations.

He says, '*You* didn't kill her. We can start from that premise ... right?'

'*I* didn't kill her,' I agree.

'But, after that confession ...' he begins, then stops.

'The police think I did.' I slip the end onto the unfinished sentence.

'They've been wrong, before,' remarks Kelly, drily.

I say, 'They'll have closed their file on the case.'

'Probably. But, it's still their file.'

'Let's re-open it.'

Kelly watches my face as he speaks. His eyes are a man-hunter's eyes; neon-blue and hard. They are eyes capable of gimleting the truth out of Ananias, himself.

He says, 'Let's get things straight, Russell. This isn't America. Over there, the private investigator has a certain standing. He's even licensed. The American police accept him. They don't love him—they don't even *like* him, too much—but, if he's honest, and if he keeps his nose clean, they tolerate him as a necessary evil.

'It doesn't work that way in the U.K. Over here, they hate private detectives. Good, bad or indifferent ... they still hate 'em. I know. When I was in the force, *I* hated private detectives. I wasn't content with not helping them ... I hindered them, as much as possible. They were blacklegs. Some of 'em—and some of 'em still *are*—lower than the villains doing time. So, we can forget the police. They won't help. More than that, they'll block us, as often as they can.'

'Which means?' I ask.

'The near-impossible.'

' "The impossible takes a little longer",' I quote.

'I know the saying.'

He tries the packed pipe for air-flow, is apparently satisfied and returns the pouch to the desk drawer.

'And money,' I say, 'has been known to buy "impossibilities".'

He nods.

He takes a fancy table-lighter from the desk top, thumbs it into flame and lights the newly-packed tobacco. It is good tobacco—not at all like Garret's thin twist—and the aroma conjures up visions of T.V. ads, and nubile young women all eager to shed their panties.

Very quietly, I say, 'A century a week, and expenses, as a retainer ... for however long it takes.'

He watches me, through tobacco smoke.

'You ... personally,' I add.

He continues to watch me, but says nothing.

'Do we have a deal?' I ask.

'Ye-es. We can, provisionally, assume we have a deal.'

'Good.' I make no attempt to keep the satisfaction from my voice. 'In that case, let's talk about corruption.'

'Ten thousand?' It is more than a question. It is an indirect, but positive, acceptance of the job. He says, 'A nice, round figure.'

'It could be more. Certainly not less.'

'How?'

'We price the job,' I explain. 'Architect's plans. Quality specifications. We view the site. We set the quantity surveyor onto the job, and work from his figures. Then, we give ourselves elbow-room—there's always unforeseen snags—and quote a price.'

'Simple?' He burns fancy tobacco, and watches for my reaction to a very loaded question.

'The make-or-break factor,' I assure him. 'I've known firms go bust—good firms—because they've miscalculated the cost of locks and knobs, on a few hundred doors.'

'As tight as *that*?'

'It can be.'

'So-o ... ten thousand?'

'Prestige jobs. There's more leeway.'

'Ye-es ... but, *ten thousand*?'

'A municipal recreation centre,' I say, heavily. 'A strong man on the council, pulling strings ...'

'Roebuck?'

'Roebuck,' I agree. 'He pushes the tender through the various committees. It's over-priced, in the first place. Then, when it's accepted, the fiddles are worked. Cheaper frames in the windows ... they look the same, but they're not. The same with doors, bricks, sanitary fittings, the various mixes—more sand than the specification demands

66

... everything! You make a little, on everything. It adds up to a lot.'

He nods, slowly. He is convinced.

I say, 'It's done. Every day. The Roebucks are around. There's a would-be Roebuck on every council.'

'As bad as that?'

'We-ell ...' I move my shoulders, and spread my hands.

His pipe is not working to his satisfaction. He encourages it with a boost from the lighter-flame.

Then, he asks, 'Your firm?'

'We don't work that way.'

'Never?'

The question is not *quite* an insult. It is a deliberate goad; the feint to the gut, which makes a bad fighter drop his guard and leave his jaw exposed.

I light a cigarette, before I explain certain facts of life. *My* life ... and the life of *my* firm.

Then, I say, 'Craftsmen. The genuine article. They're as precious as water, in the Sahara. The same with grafters ... men who exchange a good day's work for a good day's pay. I've collected them. I've coaxed them. I've coerced them. I've even bribed them. I've collected them, like a philatelist collects rare stamps. That's what's made the firm what it is, today. It's why Russell and Macks, Limited doesn't have to be spelled out in the world of building contracts. R. & M. ... that's enough. The rest fight amongst themselves for second place. We work for corporations, or companies. Sometimes, for millionaires ... because only millionaires can afford the class of work we turn out. Our sort of firm exists in every trade. Every profession. The excellence is taken for granted. Other firms don't even try to parallel.'

'Rolls-Royce,' he murmurs.

'The same thing,' I agree.

He says, 'How was it born?'

'More of a marriage than a merger.' I hold my cigarette

at eye level, and examine the glowing tip, as I talk. 'Bill Macks ran a top-class builders' merchants firm. His son died in World War II. North Africa ... trod on a land-mine. For a time, Bill went to pieces. Then—it happens that way, sometimes ... he tried to work himself to death. A form of prolonged suicide. It didn't come off. It rarely does. But the firm prospered, and Bill worked the bitter-ness out of his system. I'd taken over my father's build-ing firm. Accepted some above-average contracts, and earned a reputation. I knew Bill. We respected each other. The new firm—Russell and Macks—we-ell ... it seemed lunacy not to.'

'And, of course, it worked.'

'Until now.' I drag deeply on the cigarette, and repeat, 'Until now.'

We smoke in silence, until he thinks up the next ques-tion. It is a very simple question. Unfortunately, it does not admit of a very simple answer.

'Who could have known?'

'A dozen people.' I sigh. Then, I correct myself. 'No ... they'd keep it quiet. Four, or five, who *must* have known.'

'Who?'

'The site manager. Probably the site foreman—although, maybe not ... he doesn't spend much time in the site office. The quantity surveyor ... I can't see how he *couldn't* know. Architects. Anybody with access to the tender. Anybody capable of reading a plan drawing.'

'Macks?' he asks, softly.

I nod miserable agreement.

'But, not you?'

'I handle the men,' I say. 'We've always worked it that way. The hiring and firing. Labour problems. Wage settle-ments. Those are my problems. Bill deals with materials. Estimates. Quotations. Tenders. Nothing watertight ... we each know what the other's doing.' I check myself, twist my lips into a bitter smile, and add, 'We *did*.'

The door of the office opens, and a woman brings in a tray loaded with coffee and scones. She is early middle-aged, but without a wedding band; one of the army of dedicated 'career' types who, at their best, can make a mere man look stupid and incompetent. She pours the coffee, and passes out the plates and scones.

When we are once more alone, Kelly says, 'Roebuck and Macks. One of them—or, both of them—realised you were onto the ten thousand. One of them—or, both of them—framed you. Agreed?'

'I ... I ...' The words won't come. The truth—what *has* to be the truth—chokes me.

'You *were* framed,' insists Kelly.

I nod my head.

'You did *not* murder your wife?'

'No ... I didn't murder my wife.'

'So? It's a frame. Isn't it?'

'It would seem so.'

'Russell, if you can't accept the ...'

'All right,' I croak. Then, in little more than a whisper, 'All right. It was a frame.'

'Motive ... to put you out of circulation, before you could prove the ten-thousand-pound back-hander.'

'I ... I—er—I suppose so.'

'For God's sake!'

'I don't know,' I snarl. 'That's what I'm prepared to pay to find out. Find out ... then tell me. Let me decide, when I have facts worth some sort of a decision. Just find out ... that's all.'

Those pale blue eyes burn into my face, and laser the truth from its hiding place.

He says, 'You're a mug, Russell.'

'It's possible.'

'Somebody doesn't love you as much as you think they do.'

'That, too, is possible.'

69

'You were lucky. Very lucky. The verdict fell in face of the breeze.'

'I was innocent. So ...'

'You could have gone down. You were *meant* to go down.'

I move my head in dumb acquiescence.

'Roebuck?' he asks.

'Yes. I think Roebuck. Roebuck took the skim-off.'

'Macks?'

'It's—it's possible,' I mutter.

'Anybody else?'

'I can't think of anybody.'

'Quantity surveyors? Architects? Anybody?'

'Some of them would know ... I *think*. But they'd be sure *I* knew.'

'Good.' He strokes the lighter flame across the surface of the pipe tobacco and, between puffs, says, 'Good. Good. We're moving.'

Kelly is happy. Or, if not happy, satisfied. He has organised himself a base-line upon which he can build his enquiries. Two names. Roebuck and Macks. He has a target; he is, already, no longer groping in the dark. He doesn't know Roebuck, he doesn't know Macks, therefore he can be beautifully objective about the whole problem.

Bully for Kelly!

Me?

I know Bill Macks ... and more than 'know' him. I like him, and my feeling for him isn't far short of that of a dutiful son to a respected father. Bill Macks just might have been instrumental in standing me in that murder dock ... it is *just* possible.

But, even the acceptance of that bare possibility, brings a sour taste to my mouth.

Kelly says, 'Right. Now, let's start at the beginning. The evening of the murder. Twelfth Night, wasn't it?'

'January the sixth,' I agree.

'I know the outline. What the newspapers have been allowed to print. Now, I want to know everything ...

CHAPTER SEVENTEEN

R. v. RUSSELL.
Extract from Record of Trial.
Cross-examination of Accused, by Prosecuting Counsel.
Counsel. Did you see the car, Russell?
Russell. Yes.
Counsel. Your wife's car?
Russell. I didn't know that, at the time.
Counsel. A Triumph?
Russell. Yes. A Triumph Toledo.
Counsel. Your wife's car?
Russell. I didn't know that.
Counsel. Whose car did you think it was?
Russell. I didn't know.
Counsel. A strange car?
Russell. Yes, But ...
Counsel. Parked, on the verge, outside Yew Cottage?
Russell. Yes. Parked just by the ...
Counsel. And the nearest house? How far?
Russell. What?
Counsel. To Yew Cottage? How far to the nearest dwelling house?
Russell. Oh, about half a mile. Probably three-quarters of a mile.
Counsel. Therefore, the car—the Triumph—belonged to somebody visiting you?
Russell. Yes. Unless ...

Counsel. Go on, please. Unless what?

Russell. Abandoned. It might have been stolen, and abandoned there. It's happened before.

Counsel. Many times?

Russell. No. Just once, before.

Counsel. When you saw the car, did you think it was an abandoned vehicle?

Russell. No.

Counsel. What, then, did you think?

Russell. Well ... Nothing. I didn't think anything.

Counsel. Come, Russell. That won't do, will it? You arrive home. You find a car parked outside your gate. The nearest other dwelling is at least half a mile away. And you expect the court to believe you didn't jump to a normal conclusion? That you had a visitor?

Russell. I—I suppose so. I suppose that's what I thought. But I'd seen the glow from inside the house, and ...

Counsel. Your wife?

Russell. What?

Counsel. You realised it was your wife ... surely?

Russell. No. That's not true. I didn't know it was my wife's car.

Counsel. Who has a key to Yew Cottage, Russell?

Russell. I have.

Counsel. Who else?

Russell. The police. I ... think the police have a key.

Counsel. This other key—the key the police hold—where did that key come from?

Russell. They—er ...

Counsel. Yes?

Russell. They took it from the body of my wife. From her handbag.

Counsel. She had a key to Yew Cottage?

Russell. Yes.

Counsel. Who else had a key?

Russell. Nobody.

Counsel. By that, I presume, you mean nobody ... to your knowledge?

Russell. No. I mean nobody else had a key. Nobody!

Counsel. For the benefit of the court. How can you be sure?

Russell. It was an isolated cottage. Left, for reasonably long periods. It needed security. There was only one lock, operative from the outside. An Ingersoll. Expensive. As near pick-proof as you can get. Two keys. And a third key was only available on my personal, written authority.

Counsel. You never gave that authority?

Russell. Never.

Counsel. Therefore, two keys. Only two keys?

Russell. Yes. Only two keys.

Counsel. Your wife's car, parked at the gate?

Russell. I didn't know it was her car.

Counsel. Somebody waiting, in Yew Cottage? Somebody already there?

Russell. All I saw, at first, was the ...

Counsel. Who else, Russell? Who else, other than your wife, could gain entrance to the cottage? Who else could have been waiting?

CHAPTER EIGHTEEN

The coffee has scummed, and Kelly's pipe is cold but, now, Kelly knows everything I know. I have told it without passion, and I have told it as it happened. Without frills. Without an implied opinion.

Kelly has listened, without interruption. He has jotted down some sparse notes on a foolscap scribbling pad. He has nodded his understanding a couple of times. Other than that, he has kept a straight face.

Now, he says, 'You didn't kill her ... but she *was* killed.'

It isn't a question, therefore I do not provide an answer.

'Somebody killed her,' he continues. 'Somebody. Nice timing, too. Who knew you were spending the night at Yew Cottage?'

This time it is a question. And very loaded.

I say, 'Bill.'

'Macks?'

I nod.

'Anybody else?'

'A score of people.' It is a form of retraction. I have placed Bill directly in the firing-line and, to obscure Kelly's aim, I now surround him with a crowd of nobodies. I say, 'I mentioned it, umpteen times. Over the Christmas holidays. Office staff. Friends. It was Twelfth Night ... it was something I was looking forward to, so I mentioned it almost every day.'

'But, Macks?' insists Kelly.

'We keep in touch. It's necessary. Something might crop up ... one of us might need the other, in a hurry.'

'Somebody killed her, and framed *you*.'

'Uhu.'

'That person—whoever he is—knows you *didn't* kill her.'

'It follows.'

'And, knows *you* know you were framed.'

There is a terrible progression to Kelly's logic. A deadly progression. Prison dulls the senses, and a prolonged murder trial takes the cutting edge off thought, therefore the equation—the end-product of this progression—comes as a shock.

Kelly sums it up, beautifully.

He says, 'There's a killer at large, Russell. He's killed

74

once. He'll kill again. You, this time ... if he gets a chance.'

CHAPTER NINETEEN

It would seem I am living on borrowed time. I should be in prison ... but I am not. I should have been silenced .. but I was not. I am still free, and I am still alive ... and, in that condition, I am a perpetual menace.

To whom?

Whoever that person is, he and I have one thing in common. We are both worried. We each fear the other.

Yet, I think he is more worried than I.

I drive the Stag, automatically, and allow my mind its full freedom. It roams, and it drags strange thoughts from dark corners and, for the first time, I see the skirt-edge of the truth.

I have been kidding myself.

An hour ago, I was still kidding myself and, at the same time, kidding Kelly. I told Kelly the truth, but not the whole truth ... and I'm damned if I know why. Deliberately? Subconsciously? Because it is the one fact, in this bundle of half-lies and part-truths, which has me worried?

I thought I'd told him everything. I swear ... at the time of telling, I thought I'd told him *everything*.

Not so.

But not because I forgot ... rather, because I refused to remember. The mind of man is an odd machine. It functions like no other machine on earth. Smoothly— mysteriously ... or, not at all. It stops, it by-passes, it leap-frogs, it ignores indigestible tit-bits.

Then, suddenly, it *realises*.

And the realisation is as breath-stopping as a cold shower.

I built Kelly a bridge of words; a bridge via which he will try to pass from point 'A' to point 'B'—from speculation to precision—but a bridge which will collapse, at the first weight of enquiry, because I left out the key-stone.

Christ Almighty!

My eyes check the rear-view mirror. My foot finds the clutch pedal. My hand drops to the gear lever. Automatically ... I pull out, overtake a rumbling eight-wheeler, and flip the gear-mesh back into top. Automatically.

And my mind continues its travels.

I am living on borrowed time.

In prison, I would have been safe. Twenty years—twenty years, less remission—would have passed and, once more, I would have returned to the world. Falsely convicted, but alive.

I was not falsely convicted therefore, it seems, I must die. Kelly's logic is foolproof. Faultless. That acquittal was a death sentence.

I am suddenly very much alive. More alive than I have been for weeks—for months ... for years! The prospect of immediate death does much to clarify thought.

Thought about Bill Macks, for example.

Sir William Macks. And, of course, Lady Violet Macks. That he accepted the knighthood, in the first place, came as a shock. He isn't the only 'working-class peer'. He isn't the only 'Socialist knight'. But—good God ... Bill Macks! By his own boot-straps, to Burke's. And, good luck to him —I didn't envy him—but I was shocked. It was so out of character. So *non*-Bill Macks.

'Russ, believe me, I've met 'em. They're creeps. Parasites. They're bloody drones. Every last one of 'em.'

I've heard him say that, so many times. A decade ago, the trick was to catch him slightly tipsy, get him into a

76

talkative mood and steer the conversation along the right lines. Then, wait for it. In those days, he hated class distinction. He railed against it. He loathed it loudly, without qualification and whenever the opportunity presented itself.

Then, eight years ago, his name was included on the Birthday Honours List. Just like that. A knighthood ... 'for a lifetime of outstanding service to the building trade.'

Today, he is Sir William Macks and, in his own gruff way, he loves the subtle edge which the accolade has given him.

Men change.

They use crested notepaper where, previously, the firm's stationery gave sufficient pride.

They play at 'squire'—they slip into the role of landed gentry—where, once, they were lost without pavements, shops and the bustling life of a major city.

They grow aloof—they cultivate the trait of condescension—where, in the past, they were social animals and boisterously convivial.

Bill Macks has changed ... and, more than once.

When his son was alive, he was a happy and uncomplicated man. With the death of his son, he became withdrawn and morose. He worked himself out of this state of melancholy and, gradually, took on a hail-fellow-well-met gaiety. A fake gaiety, perhaps. Probably a façade ... but, if so, a façade which never slipped.

And now, he is Sir William Macks ... and, with the knighthood, has come another sly, imperceptible, about-face.

I hadn't noticed.

Until this moment, I hadn't noticed.

But men *do* change ... all the time.

The old Bill Macks was a complete man. He was a monstrously *honest* man, who took ridiculous pride in his own, rough-hewn honesty.

But, the new Bill Macks?—Sir William Macks? ... I am no longer sure.

Hell's bells!

I am sure about *nothing*.

CHAPTER TWENTY

Vi answers my ring.

She pecks me on the cheek, and says, 'Russ, how nice to see you. What a pleasant surprise.'

She closes the door, leads the way across the hall and, with her back to me, adds, 'Bill's in hospital. He's had a stroke ... the day before yesterday.'

There is no emotion in this addendum to her greeting. She could be ordering bread, or mentioning a change in the weather, for all the feeling she puts into the remark.

I murmur, 'I'm sorry,' and follow her into the lounge.

We settle down, with sherry, and I say, 'Sudden.'

'Quite sudden,' she agrees. 'He's had a lot on his mind, recently.'

'Really?' I keep my tone innocent, but interested.

'It happened in the afternoon.' Some degree of animation enters her voice. 'You know how he likes his mid-afternoon tea? He was having it, when the cup fell from his fingers. As unexpected as *that*.'

'How serious?' I ask.

'At his age.' She moves her shoulders. 'The doctor describes it as "mild". But what's "mild", when you're past the sixty mark?'

I am suddenly aware that she is *not* past the 'sixty mark' —nor even past the 'fifty mark' ... and that, for her age, she is a remarkably young-looking woman.

'But, not serious?' I say. 'No suggestion of it being fatal?'

'Not fatal.' She moves her lips in an enigmatic smile and, in little more than a whisper, adds, 'Unfortunately.'

I sip at the sherry, and make believe not to have heard the last word. I am shocked. Bill and Vi are supposed to have something special going for them. They personify Happy Families ... or, so the fiction goes.

We learn something new, each day.

In a very conversational voice, she says, 'His first wife warned me.'

'Uhu?'

'She knew he was keeping me. Oddly enough, we were good friends.'

'Odd,' I agree.

'She knew she was dying. She knew he'd probably marry me. She warned me.'

'I—er—I didn't know his first wife too well.'

'She was a good woman.'

'So I've heard.'

'A damn sight too good for Bill.'

This is a crazy exchange of confidences. I came here to see Bill Macks; to talk with him; to verify that he's still a man to be trusted. Instead, I am talking with his wife. About his first wife, and about the shortcomings of the man whose bed they've shared.

Meanwhile, Bill is in some hospital, somewhere, unable to defend himself ... and nobody gives a damn.

She says, 'Am I shocking you, Russ?'

'I'm—er—y'know ... a little surprised,' I admit.

'Poor old Russ.' She lifts her glass a fraction of an inch, as if in silent toast.

I give her a shamefaced grin, and say, 'I shouldn't be shocked. Not with *my* marriage.'

'Oh, I dunno.' She pouts her lips, reflectively. 'Lissa was blind to her own good luck.' She suddenly seems to remember, and adds, hurriedly, 'By the way. Congratulations upon the verdict.'

'Thanks.'

'I thought next time ...' She smiles. 'Broad arrows and mailbags.'

'So did I,' I admit. On an impulse, I ask, 'Tell me. Do you agree with the verdict?'

'Oh, come *on*, Russ.' She smiles, knowingly.

'From a purely academic point of view,' I insist.

She eyes me, then answers my question obliquely.

She says, 'I've never met a murderer, before. At least, not knowingly. It's rather—er—exciting.'

'It's bloody amazing,' I growl. 'The amount of faith the British public have in the jury system.'

'Are you saying ...'

'I'm saying I didn't kill her.' I finish the sherry, stand up and walk to the sideboard, for a re-fill, and continue, 'I'm saying more than that. I'm saying I was framed ... and that I have a nagging suspicion that Bill knew all about the frame-up.'

It was meant to shake her, but it doesn't. She drains her glass, turns in her chair and holds the empty glass at arm's length in a silent invitation. I take the glass, place it alongside my own and refill them both.

This is cat-and-mouse stuff, and not my line of country. I return to my chair, settle down and decide to do some hard talking ... and not before time.

I say, 'Ten thousand. That's a nice, round figure. It may be a little less. It may be more ... it may be a *lot* more. The chances are you know about it.'

'Me?' She acts as if she is surprised.

I put barbs into my voice, and say, 'Vi, somebody is on the take. More than that, somebody didn't want me to know about them being on the take. I smelled rotten fish. I followed the smell, and it led me to a man-sized back-hander. Bill deals with that side of the business. Bill *has* to know about it.'

'Ask Bill,' she suggests, softly.

'With ... what is it he has?'

'Cerebral thrombosis.'

'So, he has his own troubles. I'm asking you.'

'I'll have a cigarette, please,' she fences.

I play along. I light two cigarettes, hand her one and move a stand ash-tray to within reaching distance of her right hand.

I say, 'Vi, this game we're playing is a lot less innocent than Ludo. A woman's been killed. Some smart bastard has already played me for a sucker. He was unlucky. The angels smiled, and it didn't come off. But—don't let's walk around with white sticks—I'm not yet out of the wood. Ten thousand has already bought one life. It could, just as easily, buy two.'

'*You!*'

She blinks. Under the cosmetic mask, some of the colour leaves her face. She is either a fine actress, or I am touching a sensitive nerve.

'Who else?' I ask, grimly.

'Bill wouldn't do ...,' she begins.

'Let's check up on what Bill *would* do,' I interrupt. 'Twenty-four hours ago ... We-ell—twenty-four hours ago, I had an innocence which has now left me. Bill's your husband.'

'Not a very good husband.'

'I wouldn't know, and I don't care.'

'In name only.'

'That,' I say, harshly, 'is a problem, personal to your own bedroom. He trusts you. He confides in you. At the moment, I don't give a damn about his sexual prowess. I want to know about graft ... how big it is, and how long it's been going on.'

'I may not know everything.' It is a last, weak defiance.

'Share what you *do* know,' I snap.

She draws long, and hard, on the cigarette, lets the smoke drift out of her nostrils, then talks.

She says, 'This stupid firm you're so proud of. R. & M. It's a building firm ... that's all. It's in business, to make money. Something which, to you, seems to be of secondary importance. But not with Bill. Bill had to face facts. Economic facts. His job was to *make* it pay its way.'

'We don't do cut-price work. We're not interested in a cheap job.'

'Damn it! There's no such *thing* as a cheap job, these days.' The flash in her eyes and the bite in her voice ride upon her sudden anger. 'The street-corner firms ... even they don't do cheap work any more.'

I take a deep breath, then say, 'All right. I'm listening. Spell it out for me, word at a time.'

'Russ.' She leans forward a little. The anger has evaporated and, in its place is an anxiety that I should understand. 'The principles. The reputation of the firm. Things you're so sure about. They don't exist. They *can't* exist. Look ... we tender for some big project. We're not the cheapest, but we're the most reliable. That's the only thing we have to offer. Reliability. We fix a price and, come hell or high water, that price stays rock solid. No escape clauses. No ifs, no buts ... Russell and Macks quote a figure, and that figure is holy writ.'

'Which is as it should be,' I growl.

'No!' She shakes her head, draws on the cigarette, and continues, 'No, Russ ... these days, that's impossible. We'd be bankrupt, within a year. The cost of materials. The wage bill. The overheads. It's impossible to forecast the rise. Ten per cent. Twenty per cent. Russ—believe me—cement, bricks ... basics. They've all taken off into the stratosphere. Decent wood ... it's virtually unobtainable. Paint ... it's tripled in price, within as many years. Everything! Bill's tried. Believe me, he's *tried*. But, even R. & M.

have to be competitive. And what you demand can't be bought. So-o ... we submit a tender. We ease the price up, as far as we dare. Then, when the tender's accepted, we keep an eye on costs. We cut corners. We put three coats of paint, where we've contracted for four. We put a little more sand in the mix. We put blockboard—and, sometimes, veneer—where there should be grained wood. It can be done. Without necessarily making the end-product any cheaper ...'

'Oh, for Christ's sake!' I explode.

'Yes ... for Christ's sake!' She meets blast with blast. 'For Christ's sake, grow up, Russ. That cottage of yours. How the devil do you think it was paid for? With fairy gold? You're the dreamer of this firm, my friend. Bill's the realist ... he always *has* been. All right—now you've stubbed your toe against the truth, for the first time ... and, because you're you, it hurts. But it *is* the truth. Rotten, it may be. Corrupt, it may be ...'

'Corrupt, it *is*,' I rasp.

'But—damn your innocence to hell, Russ—*it's the truth*! It's part of the world. Try to change it, and you'll end up in the poor house.'

'Or, like Bill?'

She nods and, in a low voice, says, 'Yes, like Bill. With half your brain, and half your body, paralysed.'

I am sweating a little. I can feel the cold dampness on my forehead and my cheeks. I look down at the cigarette, between my fingers, and notice that the paper has a tiny stain where perspiration has touched it.

'You're suffering, Russ,' she remarks, in a soft voice.

I nod. I can't yet trust myself to speak.

'Like a kid who's just discovered the truth about Father Christmas.'

'No.' My voice is hoarse, and little more than a groan. I shake my head, and say, 'More than that. Much more than that. Like a man who's been told that his whole life has been a thing of rotten twigs and wet tissue-paper.'

'Not as bad as that ... surely?'

'Just as bad as that.' I mean it, too. I drain the sherry then, with gall in every word, mutter, 'A lousy marriage, a lousy firm, a lousy life ... bingo.'

I push myself from the chair and, holding the empty glass in one hand and the half-smoked cigarette in the other, I walk slowly to the window. Outside, the weather is its usual grey, wet self. March ... the month of misery. The lawn has yet to have its first cut of the year; it has the texture of a pony's winter hide ... rough, uneven, harsh. The starlings are bunched and strutting; the Gestapo of the bird-world ... dark-uniformed bullies, with hearts of cowards.

From behind me, Vi says, 'At least, now you know the worst.'

I hear her, but take no heed. I stare at the garden, wallow in self-pity and doubt if there will ever be another spring.

'You talked about a frame,' she says.

'I didn't kill Lissa.' I mouth the words, without emotion. Whether, or not, she believes me is no longer important. Whether, or not, anybody believes me ... I no longer give a damn.

She says, 'Bill wouldn't do that, Russ. He's a bad husband, but a good friend. He's shielded you. He's worked hard, to let you keep your illusions ... that's all.'

'He's conned me,' I choke. 'He's conned me bloody stupid. And, for how many years?'

'A few,' she admits, softly.

'Bloody good sport,' I comment, bitterly.

'Why not?' There is impatience in her tone. 'When you've a little boy, as a partner, it doesn't do to destroy his world of make-believe.'

'That's not true!'

'For God's sake!'

'It's not *true*.' I close my eyes and tighten my jaw

84

muscles. Then I open my eyes again, and mutter, 'He could have told me. He could have explained.'

'Then, what?'

'I'd have understood.'

'Like now?' she mocks. 'Like you're understanding, at this moment?'

And, the burning shame is that she's right. I *wouldn't* have 'understood'. I'd have hated the truth, then, just as much as I'm hating the truth, now. The truth, which insists that excellence is not an absolute, after all. That it is a variable. That second-best is as near to excellence as anybody can ever get ... and that, for years, we've hawked second-best, and claimed excellence.

I glance at the ceiling of solid grey cloud, which blankets a grey, and shameful, world and, for the first time, I wish to hell the verdict had gone the other way.

I wish to hell I was dead.

CHAPTER TWENTY-ONE

Bill is almost there.

He has (and more than figuratively speaking) one foot already in his grave. Half of him has stopped working; the left half of his brain, and the right half of his body. His right eye is dull, and his right cheek is as smooth, and as immobile, as wax. His right hand rests, like a withered claw, on top of the coverlet.

He is propped up in bed, and his living eye is animated by infinite sadness. Infinite pain. He is weeping, silently. The tears stream down the two cheeks and drip slowly onto the turned-down sheet. It is as if he is crying what little life he has out of himself.

I watch this man, and I am hypnotised by the weight of his misery. By the magnitude of his agony. He is a giant, brought to his knees; a good man, humbled by a world peopled by scoundrels, of whom he was never one. He represents honour, broken and beaten, by a surfeit of dishonour. Pride, shattered and made foul.

We stay in the tiny ward, for less than an hour.

We make conversation with him. No!—not 'with' him ... *at* him. He gives no answers. He merely watches and weeps. I doubt if he hears our words. I'm certain he doesn't understand them.

Bill Macks is finished.

Whether, or not, he recovers, does not affect the final issue. Bill Macks no longer exists as a man, and he is well beyond any hope of resurrection.

When we leave, his agony is matched, ounce for ounce, by my own fury.

Somebody, somewhere, is going to pay ... hurt for hurt, and tear for tear.

Somebody!

CHAPTER TWENTY-TWO

And, first, his wife. Vi. Lady Violet Macks.

She is his second wife and, at a pinch, young enough to be his daughter. I hardly knew his first wife; merely that she was a quiet, colourless woman, who died of terminal cancer, and that her death left Bill a little lonely, and a little bewildered, but not over-sad. The death had come to be an accepted fact, before its arrival and, whatever his private grief (assuming there was some) he kept it under cover without conscious effort.

At that time, Vi was his mistress. Openly, and without hypocrisy. His wife knew. We all knew. The straitlaced frowned mild disapproval, but the rest of us understood. He could have found whores—he could have fornicated secretly, in back rooms of the city—but, instead, he accepted his own carnality and chose one woman upon whom he could spend his lust ... and, perhaps, a little love.

He married Vi, and the puritans nodded their po-faced satisfaction. He did 'the right thing', after a decent interval had elapsed and, from the moment they left the Registrar's Office, it seemed a perfect match.

It was, as I now know, one hell of a deception.

Accepting that I've only heard her side of the story—assuming that she's only fifty-per-cent right—they must despise each other.

He, because he's realised, too late, that she's still what she always was ... a high-class scrubber, with her eye on the main chance.

She, because she's met her match; a man no woman can dominate ... a man who tamed her, and made her jump through the matrimonial hoop, at his bidding and with perfect precision.

The roaring rows these two must have had!

She watches me, as I walk from the bathroom. The brushed nylon sheets, and pillow-cases, are tinted blue; they give an ice-cold colour, which contrasts with her naked, animal heat. The bedclothes are rumpled, from our contortions, and one breast is bared; rounded, proud and with its nipple as hard and as erect as Vesuvius. One leg is exposed, high enough to show the first wisps of pubic hair, and the symmetry of the rump.

I walk across the carpet, and sit on the edge of the bed. I am naked, and spent.

'Darling ...' she begins.

'Not that!' My interruption is brusque, and without any gentleness. I reach a hand to the bedside table, and help myself to a cigarette and lighter. I growl, 'No endearments, for Christ's sake. It just happened to be me ... it could, and as easily, have been any other man.'

'But not as good,' she croons, softly. 'Not as satisfying.'

I light the cigarette, and it trembles, slightly, between my lips. I return the lighter to the table, and silently curse myself for the tiny feeling of pride which her words have stirred.

I can feel the cloying warmth of her smile, as she breathes, 'Was *I* good, Russ? Tell me ... was *I* all you expected me to be?'

'A cow,' I say, flatly.

'Ah, but with the right bull.' She laughs, gently. Mockingly. 'For once, with the right bull.'

The slats of the Venetian blinds slice the dawn into strips and deposit it onto the thick pile of the stone-grey carpet. I blow smoke into the shafts of light, and it billows before settling into slowly moving scarfs and layers.

She rolls onto her side, eases a hand from the sheet and walks languid fingers over the rise of my bare thigh.

'Don't,' I mutter.

'Oh, come on, Russ. Come *on* ... you can do it.'

I try to brush her hand aside, but her fingers close, a fraction of a second too soon, and I gasp as the quick pain hits, then leaves, me.

The gentle laugh comes, again, and she says, 'Careful, Russ. You'll emasculate yourself, that way.'

I twist my body, to look at her.

She has kicked the bedclothes clear and, as I watch her, she rolls onto her back, still holding me. She sprawls there, naked and spreadeagled. Enticing. Moist, and trembling, slightly. Smiling up at me, with all the age-old mockery and knowledge of a courtesan. The grandmother, and great-grandmother, of every whore who ever lived.

'Again,' she whispers. *'Please!'*

Inside her hand, she feels me harden and grow, and her smile widens in anticipation. The trembling increases. She bends her knees, and widens her thighs.

What the hell else?

What the hell *else*?

I don't remember squashing the cigarette into the ashtray. I don't remember mounting her ... coupling with her ... trying to drive the life out of her, with the fury of my own hate and lust.

I remember the clawing, and the biting, and the breathless scream, like that of a wounded animal.

And now ...

I climb from her, stand alongside the bed and stare my contempt down at her.

She meets my stare, breathes heavily, as if from a long race, and allows a thread of spittle to run from one corner of her mouth.

'God,' she whispers. 'Oh, my *God*!'

CHAPTER TWENTY-THREE

Kelly's voice has a touch of smugness. He obviously thinks he is earning his fee.

He says, 'I'm glad you rang. We have some news about the Triumph.'

'What sort of news?'

'It was her car, but she didn't buy it.'

'I could have told *you* that ... on an informed guess,' I say, nastily. 'My wife bought nothing she could wangle as a gift.'

'The sugar-daddy was Roebuck,' says Kelly.

'Aaah!'

'Does *that* surprise you?'

'It shouldn't,' I admit. 'But, now and again, the obvious can jump up and bite.'

'What's happened, Russell?' Kelly sounds suspicious.

'Happened?'

'You sound different. More cocky.'

It is one hell of a choice of expression, and I almost smile.

I say, 'Worry not, Kelly. I'm the same man ... a little harder, that's all.'

'Harder?'

'More determined.'

'Oh!'

Choosing my words carefully, I say, 'Stick to the killing, Kelly. Leave the corruption side to me.'

'Look, the two are ...'

'Just the killing,' I insist. 'Get me the name of the bastard who *should* have stood in the dock.'

I expect an argument, and I get one.

He says, 'Murder is strictly police business, Russell. We can't ...'

'Not any more,' I cut in.

'What?'

'That particular murder. The police have closed the case.'

'They open cases, and re-open cases, every day of the week.'

'Fine. That's what I'm paying you for.'

'Eh?'

'To root out good and sufficient reason *for* them to re-open the case.'

He hesitates, then says, 'Crawford won't like it.'

'Crawford,' I snap, 'can find the nearest corner, and do the other thing.'

'You certainly *have* changed,' he remarks, sourly.

'Just the killing, Kelly,' I emphasise. 'Anything else, sit on it, till you hear from me.'

I drop the receiver onto its rest, before he can start re-negotiations.

I am wearing one of Bill's dressing gowns, over a pair of Bill's pyjamas. It is arguable that I should feel guilt, but I do not. I have subjugated this bitch of a wife of his. She is, at least temporarily, under some sort of control. Her starch-stiff arrogance has, for the moment, been driven from her and she has been exposed, even to herself, for what she is. A creature of little intelligence. A thing of no depth, and little charm. A sex object. A necessary, but easily replaceable, appendage to male fornication.

Had Bill taught her this basic lesson, years ago, their marriage might have had more than a mere façade of happiness.

I have done Bill a service, therefore I feel no guilt at wearing his clothes.

She is waiting for me in the breakfast room.

The toast is done to perfection; hot, light-brown and crisp on the outside and crumbling on the inside. The butter is farm-fresh, moist and ready for spreading. I have a triple choice of marmalade; orange, lemon or grape-fruit. The coffee has a tang 'instant' variety can never boast, the brown sugar is piled high in the basin and the cream almost touches the lip of the jug.

It is a first-meal-of-the-day fit for a monarch ... or a stallion!

She watches me, for signs of approval, with doe-round eyes.

I ignore her, and begin to eat.

'Is it ...' Her voice is fawning, and filled with lick-spittle. 'Is it all right, Russ?'

She is anxious that I shall be pleased.

I chew the toast, swallow, then sip at the coffee.

I say, 'Tell me about Roebuck.'

'Roe ...' Slowly, she bends into the chair, across the table from me. She breathes, 'Roebuck?'

91

'Alderman Maurice Roebuck of The Garth.' I don't even look at her. I spread butter and marmalade and, before I pop the next piece of toast into my mouth, I say, 'Tell me all you know about the bastard.'

CHAPTER TWENTY-FOUR

R. v. RUSSELL.
Extract from Record of Trial.
Examination-in-chief of Timothy Crawford, detective chief inspector, by Prosecuting Counsel.

Counsel. And, at that time, as I understand it, you were out on another call?

Crawford. Yes, sir.

Counsel. Tell the court, chief inspector. In your own words.

Crawford. We were in a radio car. Myself, and Detective Sergeant Williams. We'd been to Skybeck. On what had been reported as an attempted shop-breaking.

Counsel. Er—'reported'?

Crawford. A nine-nine-nine call, sir. Received at Colbank police station ... that's the divisional headquarters. It turned out to be a hoax. We were on our way back to Colbank, when we received the radio message, about Yew Cottage.

Counsel. From Colbank police station?

Crawford. Yes, sir. From D.H.Q.

Counsel. Carry on, please, chief inspector.

Crawford. Yew Cottage wasn't too far out of our way. It was quicker to go straight there. Rather than go to D.H.Q. first. We arrived, at the same time as a squad car. Four of us. Detective Sergeant Williams, myself and two uniformed motor patrol constables.

Counsel. So your evidence—what you saw, and what you heard—can be corroborated, by the evidence of three other police officers?

Crawford. Yes, sir. We entered the cottage, together. Well —strictly speaking—Sergeant Williams went through the door first. I was immediately behind him. The motor patrol officers were immediately behind me. In effect, we went in together.

Counsel. Continue, please.

Crawford. There was a blaze going, in the main room. Downstairs. It was a big enough blaze—the carpets, some of the curtains and some of the furnishings—but it wasn't out of control. The Fire Service ...

Counsel. What about the Fire Service?

Crawford. The Fire Service had been notified. They were already on their way. The radio message—the one we'd received on our way back, from Skybeck—had told us that.

Counsel. Therefore, in your opinion, the fire was no great problem?

Crawford. No immediate problem. It could be contained and extinguished. Once the Fire Service arrived ... and they were on their way.

Counsel. Carry on, please, Mr Crawford.

Crawford. The accused, Russell, was in the room. He was holding a gun. A .22 sporting rifle ...

Counsel. Exhibit Number Five?

Crawford. Yes, sir. Exhibit Number Five.

Counsel. How was he holding this rifle, chief inspector?

Crawford. He—er—he had his right hand, at the point where the stock meets the breech. With his right forefinger through the trigger-guard. He was holding the barrel, with his left hand. The way you hold a rifle, when you're firing from the hip.

Counsel. The way a man would hold a rifle, should he wish to fire that rifle from the hip?

Crawford. Yes, sir.

Counsel. Or, conversely, the way a man might be holding a rifle, after he has fired that rifle from the hip?

Crawford. Yes, sir.

Counsel. Continue, please.

Crawford. That was when I first saw the body, sir. I saw Russell, first. Then, the body.

Counsel. Tell the court about the body, please.

Crawford. It was a woman. She was—she was on fire.

Counsel. On the carpet?

Crawford. Yes, sir. Curled up, on the carpet.

Counsel. Dead?

Crawford. Subsequently, she was pronounced dead, sir. By a qualified practitioner.

Counsel. Did she look dead? When you first saw her? Did you form a personal opinion?

Crawford. Yes. She looked dead. I was quite sure she was dead.

Counsel. How far from Russell was she?

Crawford. About three yards, sir.

Counsel. Was he facing her? Or, had he his back to her?

Crawford. He was facing her.

Counsel. With the rifle pointing in her direction?

Crawford. Yes, sir. With the gun pointing in her direction.

Counsel. Chief inspector, you say this unfortunate woman was 'on fire'?

Crawford. Yes, sir.

Counsel. Amplify that statement a little, please.

Crawford. She was—she was burning, sir. Her clothes were on fire. So was her hair. Her arms, her legs, her body. She was burning, sir. There was a smell of burned flesh in the room. She was burning ... that's the only way to describe it.

Counsel. Other things in the room were also burning, of course?

Crawford. Oh yes, sir. Carpets. Curtains. Some of the furniture was starting to burn.

Counsel. Chief inspector, you know what is meant by the expression 'the seat of a fire'.

Crawford. Yes, sir.

Counsel. In non-technical language, it means where a fire starts?

Crawford. Yes, sir.

Counsel. If, for example, a person smokes a cigarette in bed. If as a result of this habit, the bedclothes catch fire, and the house is burned down, the seat of such a fire would be the bed. Do you agree?

Crawford. Yes, sir.

Counsel. The seat of the fire, in Yew Cottage?

Crawford. Sir?

Counsel. Where was it ... in your opinion?

Crawford. Sir, I'm not qualified in these matters. I'm not an expert, therefore ...

Counsel. We've already heard expert evidence on this point, chief inspector. I merely want the opinion of a non-expert. A picture, if you will, of a scene. A burning room. You entered that room. You saw the fire. You reached an opinion, regarding the seat of this fire. A non-expert opinion. Nevertheless, the court would be interested to hear that opinion.

Crawford. That ...

Counsel. Yes?

Crawford. That the seat of the fire was the dead woman.

Counsel. That the fire had, in fact, started at the body?

Crawford. Yes, sir.

Counsel. A non-expert opinion, of course.

Crawford. Yes, sir. A non-expert opinion.

Counsel. But, an opinion which was, subsequently, ratified by evidence of traces of petrol and paraffin on the clothes of the dead woman.

CHAPTER TWENTY-FIVE

And now I have met Maurice Roebuck—*Alderman* Maurice Roebuck—and *Alderman* Maurice Roebuck is a 'fixer'.

It stands out a country mile.

Roebuck is a shopkeeper. He runs a moderately sized outfitters, on the fringe of the city's heart; not too classy, not too cheap and very, very ordinary. Which means, he is not legitimately loaded.

But, he surely has bread.

The Garth gave the first clue. It stands in its own three acres of immaculate gardens. It is a miniature, all-mod-con-palace, complete with tennis court and tiny swimming pool. For a small-time shopkeeper—which is all Roebuck is—it screams an affluence ten times greater than he could ever afford.

Back-handers went into the construction of this place. More back-handers pay for its upkeep.

I knew this, before I even met the owner.

The owner merely verifies my already-reached conclusion.

He wears a brocaded smoking-jacket and a cravat. He smokes man-sized cigars from an amber holder. He surrounds himself with the luxury of near-museum-piece furniture. He drinks expensive booze from expensive glassware, and gives the general impression of doing the rest of mankind a favour by being alive.

'I'm sorry,' he drawls.

'Sorry?'

'About your wife. About the death of your wife. In such tragic circumstances.'

'Oh ... of course. Such tragic circumstances,' I murmur.

We try to out-stare each other for a few moments, then he lifts his hand and tastes his booze. The hand has the usual quota of four fingers, and a thumb, and it sports three ornate rings and a wrist-bracelet.

He lowers his glass, and his smile freezes into a fixed, plastic gloss as he settles himself on a giant ottoman, alongside a giant electric fire.

'You knew her,' I say.

'Slightly,' he admits. 'We met. We knew each other ... vaguely.'

The last word is accompanied by an airy wave of his free hand.

'Slightly. But well enough to buy her a car.'

'Ah! The car.'

He nods, and sips booze, simultaneously. It is quite a trick. If I tried it, I'd have liquid down my shirt front.

'Why the car?' I ask, quietly.

'We—er ...' He looks up at me, with a man-of-the-world expression. He moves his shoulders. What the hell the shoulder-movement is supposed to mean is beyond my simple ken, but it is apparently his own brand of sign-language. Then he says, 'As I understand it, you were man and wife in name only.'

'These things happen,' I growl.

'Quite.'

'But, she had money enough to buy her own cars.'

'Ah! But—we-ell ... y'know.'

For the third time he wets his lips with liquid courage. He is worried. At the very least, he is worried ... and possibly scared.

I say, 'Roebuck, I didn't like you, even before I met you.'

'Really?' He looks surprised. Disappointed. 'I find that a little ...'

'Since meeting you, I don't dislike you any more.'

'Good. There's no real reason why we can't ...'

'I hate the bloody sight of you.'

'Oh!'

'You,' I say, flatly, 'have been having it off with my wife ... often enough, and long enough, to merit the gift of a motor car.'

'She's dead, Russell. It's past. Done with. You can't ...'

'She's dead,' I agree.

'It's—it's past. It's ...'

'And you're a liar, Roebuck.' I allow my feelings to show in my tone. I walk around the carpet, as I talk. Slowly, and without even granting this animal the courtesy of looking at him, as I insult him. I say, 'All that crap about knowing my wife ... "vaguely". You shared her bed, for a motor car. And that car was parked outside *my* home, when she was killed. And *I* damn near ended up behind bars, because certain people couldn't quite make two and two come out a nice neat four. She did things for that car, friend. I tend to wonder exactly *what* she did. I tend to wonder. Knowing *her*—knowing *you*—I could make guesses guaranteed to be within a hair's-breadth of the truth.'

'You—you don't know me, Russell. You don't ...'

'Cut it out, Roebuck.' The disgust I have for all gold-brick merchants makes my tone rough and raspy. 'She was a cow. She deserved all she got. And you know it. If you knew her well enough to buy her motor cars, you knew her well enough to know *that*. I killed her ... that's what the coppers say, and still say. I *didn't* kill her ... that's what a jury says. Either way, it isn't too important. Just that she's well on her way to hell. That's all that matters.'

After which outburst, he doesn't know what to do with his mouth, so he compromises ... he uses it as a hole into which he pours more booze.

I pause in my stroll around the carpet. I stand, within a yard of where he is sitting, and I eye a pair of crossed swords, fixed to the wall above the electric fire. They are cavalry sabres. Heavy-bladed and with man-sized grips and quillons.

I reach up, and unhook one of the sabres and, as I do so, I hear his intake of breath.

I say, 'Williamson ... the bar-keeper. How much was it worth?'

'Wh-what? I don't know what ...'

'He recognised me. He reads the more lurid newspapers ... he recognised me. He set me up. Phoned you. How much was it worth, Roebuck?'

'I—I don't know what you're ...'

'Damn it, they *knew!*' I whirl on him, and he cringes. He probably thinks I'm going to use the sabre on his dirty neck ... and he probably isn't a million light years askew of the truth. I snarl, 'Roebuck, they knew. The bastards who ganged up on me. They knew my name. Knew I was coming. They were waiting ... for *me*.'

I continue my carpet pacing. I swing the sabre, as I allow the fury of my words their full freedom. I am, I think, a little mad. If so, I have cause to be a little mad.

'Bill Macks,' I say, tightly. 'I saw him, yesterday. Ten thousand is a lot of money, scum. It buys a lot of corruption. It bought *you* ... and smashed Bill Macks beyond all hope of recovery.'

I swing the sabre, and the blade bites deep into the polished woodwork of a fine sideboard.

'It ruined an honourable firm. A good firm. *My* firm. It became the worm in the apple of that firm. Ten thousand worms ... all turning good flesh rotten. And you put them there, Roebuck.'

Another swing of the sabre's blade opens the leather upholstery of a high-backed wing chair.

'But it ends here, bastard. It ends. Here! I can take you. I can prove it. I can throw a whole shit-cart at you, Roebuck ... and most of it will stick. The firm might wobble, but that's a risk I'm prepared to take. But you? You'll do a damn sight more than wobble, my friend. You'll go under. Under ... and *out*.'

Maybe it's a Ming vase. Maybe not. Maybe just an expensive reproduction. Who cares? It was never made to withstand the slash of a sabre's blade. It shatters, and pieces fly across the carpet.

From some room, farther inside the house, I hear voices. Excited voices. Somebody has heard the din, and is on the way to investigate.

I stand in front of the trembling Roebuck, and snarl, 'That's it, scum. You're off my back ... or you're finished. R. & M. ... touch it once more with your grimy fingers, and you'll squeal. I promise! The firm. Bill Macks. Anybody who even *knows* Harvey Russell. And they'll need a mop and pail to clean you off the pavement.'

I reverse my grip on the sabre and drive it hard, through the sheepskin rug—through the expensive carpet—and into the woodwork of the floor. The blade quivers and the hilt pendulums slowly in front of his staring eyes.

I am clear of the room, via the french windows, before the owners of the voices arrive to ask all the questions.

No doubt Roebuck has the answers.

The Roebucks of this world always have answers ... to everything.

CHAPTER TWENTY-SIX

I feel good. I feel better, and more alive, than I've felt for months. Years. I drive the Stag with a style I thought I'd lost; third-gear work where, strictly speaking, it isn't necessary, merely for the angry sound of a snarling engine. In age, I am past the half-century mark. but in spirit, I am in the mid-thirties. I am prime, I am fit and I am ready and eager to meet whatever anybody decides to throw in my direction.

I perform a spot of parlour self-analysis.

I have (I decide) a fight on my hands, and I enjoy fighting. As yet, I have not positively identified my enemy; the killer who tried to smear me with his pitch. Roebuck? We-ell ... not *personally*. Any man who sits and shakes, while another man creates havoc in his ...

I enjoy fighting!

The thought does a double-take within my mind.

I grin to myself, as the truth cuts its way through the murk of doubt.

Time was, when I was what would, these days, be called a tearaway. I was feared for my temper. I was feared for my strength. I was feared for the don't-give-a-damn arrogance with which I swaggered through life.

Gradually, over the years, the steam has died. No!—not died ... been subdued. I have taught myself control. Big business has necessitated the injection of iced water into my veins, in order to cool the blood. Talk has taken over from action. R. & M. could never have been built on fist-work ... and my priority has been to build R. & M.

The change has been as gradual as it has been false. I've hardly noticed it. The required diplomacy of big business has taken over, and made me less of a man than I was. Smoother. Less direct. Less honest.

Less of a man than I was.

Less of a man than the man Lissa married.

And *there's* a thought!

I brake at a junction and, instead of heading for Yew Cottage, which was my original plan, I make for Colbank, and the police station. It is Saturday, and Crawford is a detective chief inspector, therefore the chances are he is not in his office. That doesn't matter. They'll know where he is. They'll know his home address. And I need expert advice.

I could, I suppose, ask Kelly. And, if pressed, Kelly would give me the information I seek. But Kelly has been out of the force for a number of years, and Kelly didn't police this district. Therefore, Kelly's information would not be up to date. Nor would it be as certain as the information which (with luck) I'll get from Crawford.

Crawford is my man.

The decision warms me. It is a positive decision; a deliberate movement, on my part, towards a known goal.

CHAPTER TWENTY-SEVEN

Hell knows who they get to design police stations, these days. Toy brick manufacturers, at a guess. Colbank D.H.Q. is a faceless, featureless box, filled with lesser faceless featureless boxes; it is glass, concrete and Scandinavian pine; it is square-cornered and straight-lined and could be a Bingo hall, a cinema, a Spanish coastal hotel or a fun-fair restaurant. That, in fact, it is a police station always comes as a slight shock.

The uniformed sergeant, on duty, is as rigid and as un-compromising as the building which houses him.

'No can do,' he grunts, in a flat and final tone.

'I need to see him,' I insist.

'He's off duty.'

'It's important.'

'There's a detective sergeant in the C.I.D. Office. I'll phone through, and see if he's busy.'

'Crawford,' I say, doggedly.

'Crawford is a detective chief inspector.'

'That, I know.'

'You *should* know.' For a moment, animation gleams in

the sergeant's eyes. 'He damn near nailed you, Russell.'

'But didn't.'

'Unfortunately.'

'You will, of course, deny that remark.'

'I will, of course, deny that remark,' he agrees, flatly. 'But, we both know it was said. And we both know it was meant.'

'Detective Chief Inspector Crawford ... if you please.'

'He's off duty.'

'Therefore, his home address ... if you please.'

'Russell.' The sergeant leans a little way over the counter, as if he is about to pass on certain confidential information. He says, 'They don't like being disturbed ... detective chief inspectors, I mean. They inhabit their own little world. Anything less than rape, and they don't want to know. Okay—for a while, the only copper you ever talked to was a D.C.I. ... but, for Christ's sake, that was *murder*. That's *why*. Now, unless you've killed another woman ...'

'Which I have not.'

'Unless you've killed some other woman, Crawford doesn't want to know. He couldn't care less.'

'Try him,' I urge.

'Oh, no.' The sergeant shakes his head. 'You're not the one he'll chew up. *I'm* the one he'll chew up. And not for a louse like you, Russell ... not *ever* for a louse like you.'

'What would happen,' I ask, 'if I belted you in the mouth?'

'Try it, and find out,' he invites.

'Not this time, friend.' I give him a tight, hard smile. 'Some other time ... when you're not in your own midden. Meanwhile, I'll settle for second best. Tell the detective sergeant I'm waiting.'

With some reluctance, he lifts a receiver from its rest and talks to somebody in a C.I.D. Office.

The Detective Sergeant isn't *quite* a stranger.

He was with Crawford, on the evening of the killing; he

came into Yew Cottage, helped put out the fire, and then helped with the initial questioning.

He says, 'Russell.'

There is no overt dislike in the one-word greeting. It is even backed by a slight smile of near-welcome.

He is a youngster. At a guess, not yet thirty and, no doubt, full to the brim with spit and vinegar; there is about him an air of supreme confidence which will, in time, harden into dictatorial certainty.

Nevertheless, for the moment, he is both human and humane.

He guides me into an Interview Room, sits me at a formica-topped table, then lowers himself into the opposite chair.

'Well?' he asks.

I say, 'I'd like to see Crawford.'

'He's off duty.'

'So they tell me. I'd still like to see him.'

'About what?'

'Corruption ... and murder.'

'Another *murder*?' The raised eyebrows mock me gently. 'Don't tell me it's addictive.'

'The same murder,' I growl. 'I'm innocent ... remember?'

'That,' he agrees, 'was the verdict.'

'Therefore, somebody else must be guilty.'

He purses his lips, and nods, slowly.

'I *am* innocent,' I insist.

'Crawford doesn't think so.'

'Crawford,' I say, heavily, 'has reason for that opinion. Not a particularly good reason ... but reason enough.'

He waits for what is coming next.

I say, 'Roebuck—Alderman Maurice Roebuck ... know him?'

He nods.

'A man after your own heart?' I query.

'Not particularly.'

'A necessary evil? Would you put it that way?'

'Necessary ... because we lack evidence.'

'And, with evidence?'

He answers carefully, and says, 'I'm no advocate of evil, Russell. In any man.'

'Corruption?' I murmur.

'It's an evil.'

'Roebuck?'

'I've heard rumours ... but rumours don't mean much.'

'Proof?'

I am teasing him, with single-word questions. Deliberately. I wish to sound him out and, at the same time, make him curious. I rather like the man, and I want him on my side.

He chews his lower lip for a moment, then says, 'He's a big wheel. It'll need a lot of proof to loosen his spokes.'

'Ten thousand?' I offer.

'Proof?'

'Of corruption,' I assure him. 'Perhaps of murder.'

'Y'mean ...'

'Not personally.' I smile, and shake my head. 'I don't know the going price for a killing. But, ten thousand should pay the cover charge.'

'With something to spare,' he agrees.

'Which,' I say, 'is why I want to see Crawford.'

'Not on a Saturday.' He matches smile for smile, and shake of the head for shake of the head. 'I wouldn't know where to reach him ... supposing I wanted to.'

'No?' My question calls him a liar.

'He's on the town, somewhere. Since his girl-friend walked out on him, he's tended to stalk the tiles every weekend.'

I say, 'We all have woman-trouble,' but I am a little surprised. That Crawford leans towards promiscuity comes as a slight shock.

'So-o ...' He moves his hands in a tiny, palm-spreading

motion. 'You can't have the lord mayor. Make do with the dustman.'

I hesitate, then say, 'Okay. Why not? But—for the moment—off the record.'

'Look. I can't ...'

'Off the record. Or nothing,' I insist.

This time, he hesitates, then says, 'Fine. We'll play it your way. Off the record, till I say it's *on* the record. Then, it's *all* on the record. Everything ... as from now.'

I say, 'I need names.'

'With names,' he sighs, 'which crimes *wouldn't* be detected?'

'Men Roebuck knows, and could approach.'

'Roebuck knows half the local population.'

'Villains.'

'All the villains,' he assures me, solemnly.

We are like a duo of suspicious dogs, circling each other and sniffing. Undecided whether to play or fight. This man could be my friend. He could be my ally. But he is, first of all, a copper and, before he can help me, he has to be told things ... things which, as a copper, he might use to screw up my own plans. As far as *he* is concerned, I am an acquitted murderer; a man whose immediate past makes him suspect; a man who *might* have slaughtered his wife, and got away with it.

One of us has to build a bridge.

I am the one seeking favours, therefore I make the first move towards bridge-building.

I say, 'I didn't kill my wife. Start by believing that, then the rest follows, automatically. The firm—R. & M.—we need contracts to survive. Contracts don't grow on trees, these days. Especially big contracts ... the sort a firm of our size must have. Until recently, I was naive enough to think quality brought in the contracts. I was wrong. I stumbled across the figures. Ten thousand. Grease-money, paid by the firm for a local authority project. Roebuck

fixed it. Roebuck pocketed the back-hander. My partner—
Bill Macks—arranged the deal. You can't use him as a
witness ... he's already three-quarters the way to his coffin.
But you can use his wife ... she knew. And the books of
the firm tell their own story, if they're examined closely
enough.'

I pause, and watch for reactions.

He widens his eyes and makes a silent whistle.

He says, 'Ten thousand baubles? And we can *prove* it?'

'When the time arrives,' I promise.

'Ah!'

'There is also the little matter of murder.'

'Your wife?' He adds a qualification to the question, by
saying, 'Always assuming you didn't kill her.'

'It brings up the assumption that somebody else did.'

'Who?'

'Roebuck?' I suggest, gently.

'No.' He shakes his head, sadly. 'Knowing Roebuck, I
couldn't go along with that ...'

'Not in person. By proxy.'

'All right.' He is prepared to be convinced. 'Why?'

I say, 'Ten thousand. I'm not in the know. I'm Little
Boy Innocent. Then, I stumble across some twisted arith-
metic ... which I did. I mention my discovery to certain
people—employees, of the firm ... which I did. As of that
moment, I have to be removed. Framed. Put behind bars
... somewhere where I can't talk.'

'Ve-ery drastic.' He is not yet quite convinced.

'It's me, or Roebuck,' I argue.

'And your wife?' he asks. 'Where does she come in?
Why her? Why choose her, as a victim?'

'We live apart. We live our own lives. It's been that
way for years.'

'That,' he insists, 'doesn't answer the question. Why
your wife? Why *her*?'

'She's a director of the firm ... in name only.'

'It still doesn't answer the question.'

'She might have known about the back-hander. Probably did.'

'It *still* doesn't answer the question.'

'She was ...' The words tend to stick in my throat, but I force them free. 'She was Roebuck's woman. His current spare. He bought her motor cars ... she *had* to be in the know.'

'That still doesn't ...'

'Damn it all!' I explode. 'I know my wife. She was an unmitigated bitch. Greedy. And sly. Give her that sort of information, and she'd use it. Blackmail. Anything. If Roebuck arranged her murder, he had good reason ... that much, I'm prepared to grant him. And, if she *had* to be killed, why not make it a double-header and frame me, at the same time.'

'Neat.' The tone carries gentle, but sardonic, admiration. 'It's as neat a theory as I've ever heard.'

'It could be the truth,' I say, desperately. 'It probably is.'

'The truth usually tends to be a little less involved.'

'But, if it *is* the truth?'

He nods, slowly. Not yet convinced, one way or the other.

'Crawford would accept the possibility,' I argue.

'Would he?'

'Corruption. Murder. A frame-up. He'd accept the *possibility*. He wouldn't dare do otherwise. We're talking about crime, sergeant. Big crime. It's what you're paid to sort out. Why you're here. It's the reason for ...'

'I know my job, Russell.' The interruption is touched with impatience. 'I've listened. I haven't treated you as a crank. I haven't ...'

'Crawford ...' I begin.

'Crawford,' he snaps, 'is a realist. Whatever impression he may have given you, take it from me, he's as hard as nails. He deals in facts ... period. Not theories. Not might-have-beens. Nobody earns the reputation *he* enjoys on the strength of crackbrained possibilities.'

I stand up, and in a very nasty voice, say, 'Okay, sergeant. I've talked to the monkey. Now, I want to talk to the organ grinder. Where's Crawford?'

'I wish I knew.' And now there is barely concealed disgust in his tone. 'He could share the work-load. Take some of the decisions he's here to take.'

'Meaning?'

'Meaning, I make the decisions ... because I'm *here*. If Crawford wants to reverse any of those decisions, that's his prerogative. But, pending that reversal, what I say goes. The corruption thing ... that's a complaint I'm prepared to accept, and look into. The other thing. Forget it, Russell. Between these walls—and never mind what the verdict was—*you* killed your wife ... so don't start trying to sell jelly medals in this nick.'

CHAPTER TWENTY-EIGHT

Jelly medals!

If ever a man deserved one, the name of that man is Harvey Russell. Jelly medals, tripe sashes and custard crosses ... I've earned the lot. And the hard way.

My excuse—call it an 'excuse', for want of a better word —is that the damn detective sergeant couldn't *quite* stomach the truth. Almost ... but not quite. He reached out a hand but, when his fingers were within touching distance of the possibility that even the British Police Service can stand the wrong man in the dock, charged with a major crime, he backed off. He turned, and ran. He couldn't force himself to accept fuzz infallibility as being anything less than one-hundred-per-cent.

Crazy?

Of course it was crazy, and I told him exactly how crazy it was. He, in turn, told *me* how crazy *I* was. We bandied words—harsh words, and naughty words—and, after the words, I sought action.

I had it all worked out.

Roebuck was a man of plastic; smooth, polished, but without strength. Whatever muscle he needed, he bought. So-o—come the necessity to commit murder—he hired a paid killer.

Ergo, find the killer—buy, or belt the truth out of the killer—and friend Roebuck was there, served up on toast with a scrambled egg between his eyes.

So damn easy. So damn stupid. But, after the run-in with the detective sergeant, I was furious enough to try anything and blind enough to have complete faith in whatever madness I attempted.

I drove the Stag back to Roebuck's territory, parked it and hunted out a taxi stand. I told the driver I was looking for a Saturday night on the tiles. Low-life ... the lower, the better.

He gave me an old-fashioned look.

On an impulse, I said, 'Journalism, friend. Crusading journalism. Crime, in the provinces ... that sort of thing. Not the big cities. The lesser, run-of-the-mill places. Don't tell me they're all pure.'

'Like driven slush.' He grinned.

'Okay,' I said, 'point my nose in the right direction, and let me dig out some dirt.'

It was all he needed. The prospect of reflected immortality; the vision of being able to tell his pals that he'd had a hand in some shock exposé.

He dropped me off at this place, and wished me good luck.

It was, I think, listed as a night-club. It had all the flash goofery of a night-club; subdued and coloured lighting, a stripper's stage, booze at triple-standard prices, whores of every shade, from black to white, through khaki. There was a gaming room which, at a guess, hadn't played a straight hand within living memory. There was a bar, with salted peanuts to bring on the thirst and a bar-keep to rob you of change. There was a bevy of cigarette girls, who bounced their tits in your eyes to keep you from taking too much notice of their tray-wares.

There was everything, and the hicks of this town were enjoying themselves, and paying through the nose for being sinful.

I threaded myself through the maze of tables, found an empty chair and filled it. My table-companions were three snazzy-dressed yobs, with eyes as dark, and hard, as anthracite.

I ordered whisky and ice—called it 'Scotch on the rocks' —and settled back to work out the next move.

I needn't have bothered. The next move made itself.

One of the trio said, 'First time, mac?'

He had a hard, lined face and he had the knack of talking with the very minimum of lip-movement. He had the sort of voice a frog might have ... supposing frogs could talk.

'First time?' I wasn't quite sure what his question had meant.

'Here?'

'Oh! Yes ... first time here,' I agreed.

'Like?' asked one of his pals.

I made a non-committal noise.

Number Three rumbled, 'You won't find better, out-side Smoke, mac,' and gave the remark the air of a declaration of war.

That's how it started. Three well-dressed heavies, push-ing some not-so-important conversation from behind their teeth; me throwing the talk-back at them, while we all four poured pricey booze down our gizzards.

An hour later, we were friends. We were the four musketeers; we were stoked up with jungle juice, swopping dirty stories, ogling some middle-aged grind queen who was peeling the last of her undies, on the bar-stool-sized stage ... and they were primed for the sixty-four-thousand-dollar question.

I eased it at them ve-ery gently.

'Supposing ...' I began. I treated them to a sloppy smile, then said, 'Supposing I wanted something done. How would I go about it?'

'Eh?'

The Number One of the group was called Jim—we were well beyond first-name terms ... and Jim stared at me, with narrowed eyes, and demanded some slight amplification.

'Something,' I said. 'Y'know ... something *done*.'

'Like what?'

'We-ell ... y'know.'

'Naw.' Jim shook his head in mock-puzzlement.

'Something—y'know ... not quite *legal*.'

'Bent?' Johnny—the Number Two of the trio—made it an interested question.

'Yes,' I admitted. 'Y'know ... bent.'

'That,' said Jim, pointedly, 'means you think *we're* bent. Right?'

'Not necessarily. Just ...'

'How bent?'

'Eh?'

'How bent?' Jim repeated the question. 'Us. Whatever it is you have in mind. *How* bent?'

'We-ell ...' I hesitated.

'Corkscrew? Or just slightly curved?'

I felt ants doing an Irish jig around the nape of my neck. For the first time, I wondered whether I'd grabbed a man-eater by the whiskers; whether what I was doing was a neat combination of madness and self-destruction.

I was, I decided, too far gone—I'd already committed myself beyond recall ... from now, on, it was stick or bust.

'Murder,' I said, softly.

It widened their eyes. It tightened their lips. It flared their nostrils. The tiny muscles of three faces froze then, gradually relaxed as the eyes narrowed into half a dozen suspicious slits.

By silent consent, Jim became spokesman.

He said, 'Hey, Harvey ... you're angling after a corpse job. Right?'

I nodded.

'You wanna take out a contract. Right?' he purred.

'That's what it's called,' I agreed.

'That's a hot number, Harvey.'

'Don't tell me it can't be done.'

'Did *I* say that?'

The stripper was down to her G-string. The loudspeakers blared grunt and grind music—rasping trombones, and an emphasised off-beat—and every other eye in the room was glued to the skin-show climax.

Almost off-handedly, Jim said, 'Who d'you want knocked?'

'Can it be done?' I fence.

'These days ... men can land on the moon, mac.'

'Uhu.'

'All it needs is money.'

'How much?'

'As much as you're prepared to pay. And maybe that ain't enough.'

'Who ...' I swallowed, then said, 'Who do I see?'

'See?'

'Talk to?'

'You're talking to us, mac. These things ain't rushed.'

'You can fix it?' I asked, quietly. Eagerly.

'Nothing!' This man called Jim pinned me with dark and expressionless eyes and delivered the basics of his way of life in a bullfrog voice. 'You wanna get the facts straight, mac. We're sitting here, enjoying a quiet drink, and you come along. Nobody invited you ... right? You horn in on the conversation and, next thing we know, you're talking corpse-talk. You're making funny-funny noises with that mouth of yours. We dunno who the hell you are. We ain't never met you before. But that's no matter ... out you pop, with a load of bullshit about wanting to take a contract on some poor fink. What is this, mac? You some sorta law, asking nosey questions? That it? You some sorta stupid copper?'

I said, 'No ... I'm not a copper.'

'You *sound* like a copper.'

'What the hell,' I sneer, 'is a copper supposed to sound like? *You* tell *me* ... at a guess you've heard it more often than I have.'

'Don't get tough, baby,' growled Number Three.

'Or?'

And that, too, was a stupid, come-back question. I knew the answer to 'Or?'. With a certain brand of animal, there's only the one answer. Pain and trouble ... what else?

But, I was in over the neck and I was being hustled. And, all my life, I have had a rooted objection to being hustled.

Jim straightened up from the table. His two buddies followed his lead.

He stared down at me and, in a soft voice, said, 'This company's turned sour, mac. It ain't fit for decent men. We're leaving ... and you'll be wise not to follow. Okay?'

They edged their way, Indian-file, between the tables and left. I sat there, toying with my glass, lighting a cigarette, listening to the background buzz of Saturday-night, tanked-up chatter.

About fifteen minutes later, the waiter stopped at the table.

'Mr Russell?' he asked. 'Mr Harvey Russell?'

I reluctantly accepted ownership of the name.

'You're wanted on the phone.'

'Not me.' I shook my head. 'Nobody knows I'm here. It must be some other ...'

'You, sir,' insisted the waiter, and there was an innuendo in the words I couldn't miss. He jerked his head, and added, 'Past the bar. Into the foyer. The kiosk's on your right.'

I found the kiosk, the phone was off the hook and, when I let the party at the other end of the line know I was listening, a voice said, 'I hear you're looking for a broker.'

'A what?'

'A broker.' It was a man's voice, but muffled. I guessed that a folded handkerchief was being held at the mouthpiece. The voice continued, 'You want insurance, you go to an insurance broker ... right? You want what *you* want, you come to a guy like me. I'm a broker, Russell. I'm here to be used ... if you want to use me.'

'It's possible,' I admitted warily.

'It either *is*, or it *ain't*. If we meet we talk business ... we don't socialise.'

I tossed a mental coin, but didn't wait to see which way it fell.

I said, 'Okay. We meet.'

'You know this town?' the voice asked.

'Not much.'

'Okay, listen. Leave where you are. Turn left. There's a bridge, over the canal. Steps down, to the towpath. Walk along the towpath—about five hundred yards—there's a boat moored. The lights are on, in the cabin. When you get there, stand on the towpath and light a cigarette. Got that?'

'Left from this place,' I repeated. 'The towpath. A moored boat, with its cabin lights lit. I light a cigarette.'

The voice said, 'Be seeing you.'

The phone went dead.

And, as I replaced the receiver, every instinct in me told me to run for it. Red lights and danger bells were having a ball inside my skull ... but, what the hell! That damn detective sergeant had forced me into this situation and, having struck some sort of oil, it seemed crazy not to keep on drilling.

I should have followed instinct ... but, whoever *does*?

The towpath was dark. The yellow street lighting of the town gave an ochre glow to the roof-top sky-line, but the water of the canal was pitch and I had to keep my head lowered in order to check that my feet didn't stray from the hard-trod earth of the path.

This was my second visit to this town; my second attempt to blast some of the truth from its funk-hole.

It was a re-run of that first visit.

For the second time, I was jumped. For the second time, I was clobbered.

This time ... *hard*!

CHAPTER TWENTY-NINE

Which is why I deserve a jelly medal.

Which is why I am wrapped in bandages, horizontal in a hospital bed ... and hurting like the very devil.

I could, I suppose, feel sorry for myself. I could look up at that off-white ceiling, turn my head and look at those floral-designed screens, sniff the carbolic-and-ethyl stench of this hospital ward, taste the sandpaper sourness of a digestive-system overloaded with dope and wallow around in a nice, warm ocean of self-pity.

That, I could ... and so easily.

These last few weeks of my life have been very hard to live. They have been painful. Even frightening. I am receiving the message, loud and clear ... that I am unloved, unwanted and superfluous.

'Better?' asks Crawford.

'I hurt,' I say, bitterly. 'I hurt all over. I think they must have driven a steam-roller over me.'

'They?'

'Whoever. Men from outer-space, for all I know.'

'That's a pity,' he says, sadly. 'A description. Anything. We could be trying to trace them.'

It is a short exchange, but tiring. I have already told a uniformed constable all I know. The night-club, Jim and his two cronies, the call to the telephone and the stroll down the canal bank. The fundamentals. Not the 'whys'—not the 'wherefores' ... but enough to drape some sort of flesh around whatever report the constable was required to make.

I do not feel like doing an encore for Crawford's benefit.

I murmur, 'I've given your man the details. All I know.'

'I'll ask,' he says. 'They might let me have a copy.'

I gather my energy, roll my head to look at him, and croak, 'Don't waste too much time, Crawford. Start with Roebuck. He's the puppeteer.'

'Knowing it ... *proving* it.' He shakes his head, slowly.

'I'll prove it,' I promise, softly. Savagely.

'Maybe.'

As the dope-clouds gather under my skull, I mutter, 'With proof—without proof ... he'll wish to hell he had. *He'll wish to hell he had.*'

Crawford asks questions.

I don't answer, because I hear the questions as distorted words. Words arriving from an echo-chamber. Meaningless words—meaningless questions ... and, in my present, scrambled-egg state, the answers would be equally meaningless.

CHAPTER THIRTY

It is Monday, and I hurt a little less than I did yesterday, when Crawford paid his respects at the bedside. I have been moved into a side-ward; a single-bed room which, at least, gives me some semblance of privacy.

My Monday-morning visitor is Kelly.

He stands around, waiting until the hatchet-faced nurse fixes new dressings and, despite her scowl of disapproval, he smokes his pipe and earns his retainer by keeping quiet and having patience.

The nurse rolls her trolley out into the corridor, and leaves. Kelly carries a tubular steel chair from its position, alongside the window, and sits alongside the bed.

He wastes no time on preliminaries.

He says, 'Twelfth Night. Roebuck spent the evening at home ... alone.'

'The Garth?'

He nods.

'Who says?' I ask.

'We've asked around. Take it from me. *That's* where he was.'

'Alone?'

Again, he nods.

'Which means,' I say, 'he maybe *didn't*.'

'If you mean witnesses ...'

'I mean witnesses.'

'No witnesses. He's a divorced man. He lives alone—except for a few day servants ... therefore, no witnesses.'

I smile, knowingly.

'Don't jump to conclusions, Russell,' he warns.

'You can't be sure,' I remind him. 'Without witnesses, you can't be one-hundred-per-cent sure ... so, *you're* jumping to conclusions, too.'

He inhales pipe smoke, exhales, then growls, 'It's arguable.'

'Very arguable,' I murmur.

'Macks ...' he begins.

'Forget Macks.'

'You wanted ...'

'Macks is a dead man. All he lacks is a funeral service.'

'His wife ...'

'I'll take care of his wife.'

'Russell.' He takes the pipe from his mouth, and uses the stem as a pointer. He prods the air, in the direction of the bed. 'It may have escaped your notice, but you're in no condition to take care of anything ... or *anyone*. All told, you've about thirty stitches in different parts of your body. Discounting a couple of cracked ribs. Discounting a dislocated shoulder blade. Discounting two broken fingers. Discounting concussion. Discounting ...'

'I know! Discounting Christ knows how many cuts, bruises and contusions. I've had a thumping. Don't tell me.' I check my rising temper and, in a calmer voice, continue, 'Kelly, I'm touching a nerve, somewhere. It's obvious. Whatever it is—whoever's worked this set-up ... I'm near enough to be dangerous. I'm within hitting distance of the real murderer.'

'Oh, my word.' Kelly's expression shows mild sarcasm.

'What's that supposed to mean?'

'*You're* within hitting distance of *him.*'

I manage a wry grin. What else? Here am I, a bag of aches and agonies, and I choose a bloody stupid expression like that. As the boxer remarked to his second ... 'Keep your eye on the ref. Somebody's knocking hell out of me.'

The stupidity of the expression—the down-to-earth

gumption of Kelly—tends to set my own personal world on a more even keel.

I ignore the stabs of pain and, with my good hand, I reach for cigarettes from the bedside table. I light one, enjoy the solace of good tobacco smoke and, thereafter, talk in a more rational manner.

I say, 'Concentrate on the corruption side of things, Kelly. Nail Roebuck for *that*. Him, and anybody else who's in on the act ... other than Bill Macks. Leave Bill out of it, as much as possible. But get everybody else.' I pause, then very deliberately say, 'Smash the firm, if necessary. We can start at the bottom again, and build up.'

'And the murder?' he asks.

'My pigeon.'

'Dangerous,' he warns, sombrely.

'Twice,' I say, gently. 'There won't be a third time.'

'But, if there is?'

'If there is, I deserve it. Add the cost of a wreath to your account.'

CHAPTER THIRTY-ONE

And this, my sixth day in hospital—the day of my discharge—is a day of worry. A nagging day. A puzzled and frustrated day.

Because I know the answer.

Damn it to hell, and back, I *know* the answer. I know it ... but can't quite catch it. It is there, like a Will o' the wisp, but I can't close my fingers around it.

For almost a week, I've back-tracked, re-trod, examined and re-examined every move since the evening of the murder. Every word of those interviews. Every question, and every answer, of the trial. Every move I've made, since the acquittal.

And, it's *there*!

Hidden among the brushwood of inconsequentialities.

CHAPTER THIRTY-TWO

R. v. RUSSELL.

Extract from Record of Trial.

Cross-examination of Accused, by Prosecuting Counsel.

Counsel. May we now turn our attention to the murder weapon? Your gun, Russell?

Russell. Yes. It was my gun.

Counsel. A Remington?

Russell. Yes. A Remington 'Gamemaster'. Twenty-two bore.

Counsel. Quite. With a four-shot magazine, and a slide action re-load mechanism. Exhibit Number Five, in fact.

Russell. Yes.

Counsel. A dangerous weapon?

Russell. It was treated with respect.

Counsel. Nevertheless, a dangerous weapon?

Russell. In the wrong hands ... yes.

Counsel. Where did you keep this rifle, Russell?

Russell. In the cottage.

Counsel. Whereabouts in the cottage?

Russell. In the wardrobe. At the back of the main wardrobe.

Counsel. Hidden?

Russell. Yes. I suppose you could say hidden ... for safety's sake.

Counsel. You knew where it was hidden, of course. Who else knew its hiding place?

Russell. Lissa. My wife. I've had the gun a long time. I've always kept it at the back of the wardrobe.

Counsel. Your wife knew?

Russell. Yes.

Counsel. The dead woman?

Russell. Yes.

Counsel. Who else knew?

Russell. Nobody ... I don't think.

Counsel. In fairness, I must ask you to consider the answer to the question, Russell. Who else, other than your wife, knew that you kept this rifle hidden away, at the back of a wardrobe?

Russell. Nobody. To the best of my knowledge, nobody else knew.

Counsel. May we now concentrate our attention upon the moment when the police arrived at Yew Cottage. Where were you, at that time?

Russell. In the main downstairs room.

Counsel. With the body?

Russell. Yes. I hadn't yet had time to ...

Counsel. Just answer the questions, Russell. When the police arrived, you were in the main downstairs room of the cottage? In the same room as the murdered woman?

Russell. Yes.

Counsel. Facing where she lay?

Russell. Yes.

Counsel. Will you please tell the court what you were holding, at that moment?

Russell. The rifle. I'd just ...

Counsel. You were holding the rifle?

Russell. Yes.

Counsel. The rifle, from which had been fired the bullets which had killed your wife?

Russell. I'd just picked it up. She was on fire, and I saw the rifle, so I ...

Counsel. I will repeat the question, Russell. Were you facing the dead woman? Were you holding your Remington rifle? And is that rifle the weapon from which was fired the three bullets which killed your wife?

Russell. Yes, yes, yes. But I didn't ...

Counsel. Thank you, Russell. No more questions.

CHAPTER THIRTY-THREE

The Merc rode smoothly. It was a more pricey car than the Stag, and much of the extra cash paid for comfort and quietness.

I am glad the Merc rode so well. With a less lush car, I would not merely ache. I would be in real pain. As it is, I am merely uncomfortable, and a little wobbly.

'Feet up.' Vi stoops and gently swings my feet onto cushioned luxury. She eases off my shoes and smiles as I wiggle my toes. 'Better?' she asks.

'Nice.' I return the smile. 'You can drive well.'

'Bill hasn't driven for years.'

'Oh!'

Mention of Bill Macks brings on a feeling of guilt. I am in his house, being tended by his wife. Tonight, I shall sleep in his bed ... again, in the company of his wife. The puritanical streak within me jumps up, and bites, at the realisation. I am of an age—of a generation—of a stratum of society—which still believes in sin. To whom marriage vows have meaning.

I say, 'How is Bill?'

'The same.'

The way she says it makes me almost sure. Since she visited him, with me, she hasn't been near his bedside.

I let it pass, without comment and without question. What I don't know—what I'm not sure about—won't worry me.

She leaves the room and returns carrying a tray holding black, sweet coffee, laced with brandy. It tastes good, and we sip in comfortable silence for an uncommonly long time.

Thoughts jostle, like a sale crowd, through my mind. Thoughts without cause, and long-gone memories. Unimportant ... but, at the same time, *very* important. Memories which add up to a man's life. My life.

Today is Friday and Friday, like every other day of the week, has its own special flavour. *Had* its own special flavour ... once upon a time.

Friday. Pay-day. The wage packet, sealed and with the exact amount carefully inked across its surface. Handed to me, by my father. Solemnly, and with the tacit understanding that this was the sum total of my worth; that I was a workman, like the others ... and, that being his son put not one more penny into the packet.

And the packet handed, unopened, to my mother. The *two* packets—my own, and my father's ... because he never made rules he, himself, didn't keep. The opening of the wage packets. The counting of the notes and the coins—the pounds, the shillings and the pence—and the return to us of our respective 'spends' ... our touch of independence, and the true worth of a week's work.

Friday. The touch-paper for the weekend. The evening shave. The 'glad rags'. The slicked hair. The jingle of a filled pocket.

And my father's growled instructions—every—week— every Friday, every Saturday and every Sunday ... 'If you're drunk, don't come home.'

In those days, and by my present bank balance yardstick, I was little more than a pauper. A motor car was an unheard-of luxury. A fortnight at Blackpool was a millionaire's holiday.

But there was happiness there.

Or, was there?

Is it just nostalgia? Do I, and every other human animal, erase the bad times of the past from our memories, and look over our shoulders at a rose-tinted lie? Didn't it *ever* rain? Weren't we *ever* miserable? Didn't we *ever* feel like throwing in the sponge?

Or, does misery and defeat only come with age?

Vi interrupts my brown study, with, 'A penny for 'em.'

'They aren't worth a penny,' I say, softly. Bitterly. 'They aren't even worth accepting as a gift.'

'As bad as that?'

I shake the memories from my mind, lean forward to return the cup to the tray, and say, 'Let's talk about Lissa.'

She looks surprised.

'You knew her,' I say.

She nods.

'Better than most people. You were friends ... even after she'd left me.'

'We were good friends,' she admits.

'Okay. Tell me about her.'

'What?'

'Everything. What I don't know. Things I shouldn't know ... things I ought not to know.'

'That's a big order.' She smiles.

'We've all day. Neither of us is going anywhere.'

CHAPTER THIRTY-FOUR

And now ...

I think I know Lissa.

I have called her greedy, and I will not retract that opinion. She was greedy. Greed was a vital part of her make-up. Greed, in all its aspects. Greed of possessions, greed of power, greed for affection ... yes, even greed to be loved. It was a disease. She wanted everything. And, she could never understand the basic truth ... that to get *anything*, it is necessary to give.

Lissa gave nothing.

She grabbed, and she continued grabbing. She never once opened her fist to allow some little thing she held to fall free.

This greed disgusted me. It still disgusts me. I am trying not to, but I still find it fundamentally inexcusable.

But—we-ell, perhaps ... now I know there might be a reason.

Nevertheless, I say, 'Oh, come on! Not *Lissa*.'

'Do you know women?' asks Vi, sombrely. 'Do you know *anything* about women?'

'Not many,' I admit.

'No ... I don't mean physically. I don't even mean personally. I mean women, as a whole. Women, as opposed to men. You know men—you're a good judge of character, as far as men are concerned ... but do you know *women*?'

I say, 'They have minds. They have bodies. They're not unique. They're each different ... but they're *people*. I treat them as people. To do less would be condescending.'

'People ... agreed. But peculiar people. Special people.'

'No bra burning?' I mock, gently.

'Russ ... I'm serious.' She curls her lips, and continues, 'The Lib crowd. They're pathetic creatures. Women don't need equality. They already have superiority. Any woman, worth the name, has the world between her thighs ... and knows it.'

'Ah, but that's not the brand of equality—or superiority —the Lib crowd hawk.'

'It's the only brand that matters. Who the hell wants to be a stockbroker? Who the hell wants to be a judge? Or a preacher? Or an airline pilot? Who the hell *wants* to *be* those things?'

'Some people,' I murmur. 'But, we are discussing Lissa.'

She pauses, as if to gather the words, and get the facts in order, then she talks, and what she says shocks but, at the same time, makes sense. It explains things. It explains Lissa.

She says, 'We have this in common—Lissa and I— we've no kids. Maybe we're both barren ... the curse of the Old Testament, remember? Maybe it's in the blood. The shame of childlessness. We're animals, at heart, and the female animal's job is to multiply. To continue the species. Our only genuine excuse for living ... and, if we *can't.* We can shrug it off. We can be blasé about it. We can even make snide remarks about big families. But, I wonder ... are we kidding ourselves? Are we distracting attention—even our own attention—from our own inadequacy?

'Maybe we are. It's a terrifying thought. Especially to a childless woman. But, it's possible ... more than possible.

'Figuratively speaking, we come out in spots. Have you ever noticed? A childless woman always seems to be a little deformed. Not physically deformed—I don't mean that ... but wounded, mentally. Short-tempered. Irrational.

Intolerant. Spots—blotches ... as if child-bearing's a cleansing process, and something we've never experienced. As if our blood's still a little unclean.

'With Lissa, it was insecurity. Does that surprise you? That she, of all people, always felt insecure? Despite all the things you gave her—despite the cash, and the home, and the clothes, and the good life ... despite it all, she was insecure. No kids ... see? Nothing to interest her, in her old age. No children. No grandchildren. Only years piling on top of years. Middle-age. Then, old age. And few women improve with age. Men tend to ... but not women. She was scared. Scared of age, scared of illness, scared of death. Think about it, Russ. To be frightened of the rest of your life—*of the rest of your life* ... that's one degree of fear no man ever touches. It's reserved for women like Lissa.'

'Insecurity?' I ask although, even now, I don't fully understand. 'Is that what you mean, when you say she felt insecure?'

'That's part of it.' She nods. 'With another man—with a man who gave her what you gave her, but didn't put her in second place to his work—it might have been different. But the firm was your first love. You never pretended otherwise.'

'The firm gave her what she wanted.'

'No ... it only gave her comparative wealth. It didn't make her feel wanted. It didn't give her that warm feeling —the feeling that you're indispensable ... the feeling every woman craves. Kids give that feeling, and it's called mother-love. Women without kids need the feeling, too. And they can only get it from their husbands.'

'Bill ...' I begin.

'Bill,' she interrupts, almost harshly, 'knows damn-all about it. His first wife had a son. I've nobody ... and Bill's too old a husband to be a child-substitute.'

'Poor old Bill,' I murmur.

'Poor old Lissa,' she replies. 'If you've tears, shed 'em for *her*. You didn't know it, but you helped her well on the way to a very personal madness. She did things ... You wouldn't believe.' She closes her mouth, then changes her mind and says what she obviously wasn't going to say. She says, 'Lissa sold her shares. You didn't know that, did you?'

'Shares?' For the moment I don't understand.

'In the company. In R. & M.'

'Good God!'

'Shocked?'

'Good God, of course I'm shocked. She'd—she'd no right ...'

'Oh, yes. She'd every right. They were *her* shares. She'd every right ... and without notifying you.'

'She needs two ...'

'Two fellow-directors.' She ends the sentence for me. 'The articles of the company. "Any director may dispose of his, or her, shares, with the sanction of a majority of his, or her, fellow-directors." She had that sanction. Bill and myself. As usual, you weren't there. It wouldn't have mattered. You'd have been out-voted. She had *every* right.'

I think I could have forgiven most things. I think I could have understood the base-rock loneliness of a child-less wife ... a thing which, even suppose Vi has gilded the lily a little, is something to which I've never given previous thought. I think I could have understood that loneliness—*tried* to understand it—and, from the loneliness, the feeling of insecurity, the grabbing and the greed.

Until this moment, I was prepared to understand. I was on the point of *trying* to understand.

But, no more!

If Lissa had no child, so be it, but *my* child was R. & M. ... was, and still is. And she has sold part of my child to some stranger; to some get-rich-quick share-snatcher who will, no doubt, carve that part into lesser parts and scatter those parts to others of his kind.

'Bill must have known ...' I begin, harshly.

'Yes, Bill knew.'

'In that case, why didn't he ...'

'Why didn't *you*?'

'What?'

'This firm. This company.' She is suddenly angry with me. Her face colours, and her eyes flash. 'It's not a plaything. It's not a toy. It's not a vehicle for the personal aggrandisement of Harvey Russell.'

'Who the hell said it ...'

'You *act* as if it is. You've always acted that way. Board meetings. Shareholders ... and the Annual General Meeting. When was the last time you graced one of them with your presence?'

'I left that side of things to ...'

'To Bill. To *anybody*. You were too busy building bloody great monuments to your own ego to bother about such down-to-earth things.'

'Somebody has to be on the ground,' I argue.

'You are,' she says, furiously, 'hell's own nuisance. D'you know that? The men hate the sight of you. Like all good workmen hate the sight of a boss who's forever breathing down their necks. Something you've never considered, of course. Y'know what? ... taking everything into consideration, you've been more of a liability to the firm than you've been an asset. You wouldn't touch the desk-work. You interfered with the building-work. Taking everything into consideration, you've been an infernal nuisance. R. & M. ... it's what it is *despite* you, not *because* of you.'

CHAPTER THIRTY-FIVE

She's wrong, of course.

Christ Almighty, she *has* to be wrong!

It's like saying the Austin motor car didn't *really* need the effort of Viscount Nuffield. It's as stupid as that!

It is Friday, once more and, for a whole week I've wrestled with the possibility that what Vi said was the truth. That it, at least, contained *some* truth.

It is true (for example) that I'm no paperwork artist. That committees, and committee-procedure, are things I abhor. That I've always left that side of things to Bill ... and to the small army of desk-experts which a firm like R. & M. must employ. I don't like arguing ... probably because I'm incapable of arguing in a quiet, civilised manner. I prefer to make personal decisions, without having to either explain or justify those decisions. I accept responsibility and, having accepted that responsibility, I give orders and expect those orders to be carried out.

That much is true.

It is also true that I am happiest when I'm out on a site, somewhere. I belong to the grassroots of any project; I like to see it grow, from lines on an architect's plans, to a three-dimensional structure which captures its own beauty and its own majesty ... a beauty and a majesty far beyond the vision of any planner.

There are truths which I accept—truths of which I am not ashamed—but these truths are not, of themselves, evil. They are not, of themselves, weaknesses. Indeed, in any other man, I would count them as strengths.

Why, then, can this woman twist truth, wrap it in

doubt and present it as something of which I should be ashamed?

Women's guile, perhaps? Her own warped way of repaying me, for exposing her for what she is? The truth, made to do an about-face, in the name of tit-for-tat?

This woman—this Lady Violet Macks—is a tart. She is an energetic bed-companion ... period! She is a fornicator ... period! She is a slut ... period!

She is ... She is ...

'She's wrong, of course,' I growl.

'I wouldn't know.'

Kelly doesn't know, nor does Kelly care. Kelly, it would seem, is a little impatient with my conscience-problems, and does nothing to hide his impatience. He is a very practical man. Abstract problems leave him unmoved.

We are, once more, in his office. For the first time, since I left the hospital bed, I have driven a car; the Merc which, because of its automatic gear-change mechanism, was not hard to handle, despite the dressings on my broken fingers. It is (I suppose) a weekly progress report. Kelly telephoned, asked for the get-together, and I agreed to come to his office ... if only to rid myself of the cloying sexuality of Bill's wife, for a time.

He smokes his pipe, leans back in his desk-chair, and says, 'This isn't a confessional, Russell. You're paying good money.'

'Nevertheless ...'

'Your private life isn't my concern.'

'If I'm what she says I am ...'

'It still isn't murder. It's a long way short of corruption.'

I take his point. I sponge the problems of self-analysis from my mind, and concentrate upon more important things.

He says, 'Which d'you want? The murder, or the corruption? Or both?'

I look puzzled.

'Conflicting instructions,' he explains. 'First, it was to concentrate upon the murder. Then to concentrate upon the back-hander. You're paying. So, which? Or, is it both?'

'I—I hadn't realised.'

'It happens.'

'Does it?'

'Clients ... they all tend to sweat a little. First interview. First couple of interviews.'

'Really?'

I doubt whether I like this arrogant ex-cop. As he has just reminded me, I am paying—and good money—and what I am *not* paying for is this annoying brand of soft-centred condescension.

He puffs pricey tobacco smoke, and says, 'They're all the same.'

'Is that a fact?'

'They usually have something to hide.'

'Do they?'

'Otherwise, they'd go to the police. They come to us, because they only want to tell one side of the story. Their side. In a police station, they'd have to tell both sides.'

'Is there another side?' I ask, softly.

'To yours?'

I nod.

'The corruption thing,' he grunts, bluntly. 'You're either innocent, or monumentally stupid. It's been going on for a long time.'

'You've already dug *that* far?'

'We've asked questions ... that's all. Everybody seems to have been in the know. Except you ... if you're to be believed.'

I get a hollow, empty feeling in my gut, and say, 'Try it for size, Kelly. Try believing me.'

'You *didn't* know?' He looks mildly surprised.

'It has to be possible. It happens to be true.'

He takes the pipe from his mouth, widens his eyes, blows out his cheeks and shakes his head.

'Monumentally stupid?' I growl.

'They're not going to believe you.' He continues to shake his head.

'They didn't last time.'

'This time, they *won't.*'

'You sound bloody sure,' I say, sourly.

'A lot of people in the know ... and they all thought *you* knew.'

'Oh, for Christ's sake!'

'They *still* think you knew.'

'Would I have kept quiet?' I protest. 'Would I have just sat there, and ...'

'They did. And it's not a subject for polite conversation. People know these things. They keep their mouths buttoned. It's their job, Russell—the firm that pays 'em ... they think twice, before blabbing.'

'I did *not* know.' I grind the words from behind clenched teeth. He has to believe me, if only because I'm speaking the truth.

He shoves the pipe back into his mouth, talks around the stem, and says, 'Look at it this way, Russell. The firm's on the fiddle. You're a partner—the leading partner ... your name comes first. Now, who the hell's going to believe you *didn't* know?'

'Very few people,' I admit, grudgingly.

'Nobody! I believe you, because I happen to think you're a prize idiot ...'

'Well, thank *you.*'

'... but, who the hell else? Roebuck'll certainly drop you. He'll swear you knew.'

'His word, against mine.'

'For a long time. And, more than one Roebuck.'

'Eh?'

'More than one,' he repeats, pointedly. 'Just about every

really big contract you've hooked, within the last seven years, or so. There's been a string-puller. A pay-off. Roe-buck, himself, more than once. Others. That firm you're so bloody proud of ...' He grins, sardonically. 'It's had to work fiddles, to pay for *other* fiddles.'

'Oh, my God!'

'Something somebody once said about "pride" and a "fall",' he murmurs.

I grab myself, and do not go through the ceiling.

I whisper, 'You'll not believe this, Kelly, but I really loved that damn firm.'

'Oh, I believe it. Love, too, has an effect on the eyesight.'

'So? What do we do?' I croak.

'You tell me.'

I run my tongue around my lips, and swallow to rid myself of the dryness in my throat.

Then, I say, 'R. & M. It comes first. Number One Priority. Who the hell goes down, the firm keeps its head above water. It stays clean.'

'*Stays* clean?' The lift of the eyebrow mocks me.

'All right! It *becomes* clean.'

'Meaning, we go for the corruption angle?'

'Everything,' I snarl. 'Everybody. Every last brass far-thing.'

'It'll take some proving.' He places his fancy pipe across the rim of a heavy glass ash-tray. Carefully. Slowly. As if either the pipe, or the ash-tray, would shatter at a rough touch. He leans back in his chair, links his fingers across his lap, and continues, 'The information's there ... it usually is, in these cases. Information, but very little proof. Fraud's a hell of a thing to bring home to roost. The "ele-ment of doubt"—a thing you know something about ... it takes some shifting. The Fraud Squad boys *might* be able to do it.'

'Not the police,' I snap. 'Not until we can hand it to them ... signed, sealed and wrapped in pink ribbon.'

'Look—they have the ...'

'Not the police! I clean the mess from my own door-step.'

'They already know, of course,' he observes, mildly.

'All right. I've hinted. I've ...'

'Not just you, Russell. I mean they *know*. Lay your life on it. That they've known, for a long time.'

'In that case, why the hell haven't they ...'

'Knowing. Suspecting. Proving. I could make your nails curl.' He smiles a quick, but not very pleasant, smile. 'If crime detection was based upon mere "knowledge".'

'Roebuck?' I breathe.

'They'll know all about Roebuck. They'll be beavering away, collecting evidence ... again, lay your life on it. They'll be paying out the rope. Letting him feel safe.'

'*To commit murder?*' I explode.

Kelly lifts the pipe from the ash-tray. He holds it in his fingers. Fiddles with it. Stares at it, in silence, for a few moments, then talks to it.

He says, 'You could be wrong, y'know.'

'Wrong?'

'It happens.'

'Y'mean ... there hasn't *been* a murder?'

'Don't be stupid.'

'All right ... I'm stupid. Unscramble me.'

'Two crimes,' he muses, at the pipe. 'Time. Circumstances. On the face of things, they're linked. Maybe even two aspects of the same crime ... but *are* they? It happens, Russell. Trained minds have tripped up, before now. Two *separate* crimes. A murder. A fraud. We've taken it for granted there's a connection.'

'For Christ's sake! There has to be a ...'

'There doesn't *have* to be.' He looks up from the pipe, and stares me in the face with those neon-blue eyes. He says, 'There's no law of nature which insists that there *has* to be.'

It is a little like surfacing, from deep water. You gasp for air, and your vision clears; you shake your head to clear the last droplets, and you suddenly see, beyond the end of your nose. You see contours. You see colours. You see distant shapes. In that split second, you realise how blind you've been ... and you *see*.

There is a silence. It tiptoes along, for a full half-minute. The office clock ticks off its heart-beats, and we each wait for the other to speak.

I break the silence.

In a voice which I hardly recognise as my own, I say, 'We split the load. You handle the corruption. I'll handle the murder.'

'You'll handle the ...' His eyes widen as he begins to voice his objections.

'This.' I hold up my left hand, with its taped and broken fingers. 'This ... and a lot of other hurts to keep it company. Don't tell me *this* isn't linked in with the killing. It *has* to be. I was asking specific questions when this happened. Specific questions, to specific people. Nothing to do with back-handers. Everything to do with murder. I was getting too damn close for comfort.'

Kelly nods, solemnly.

'My pigeon,' I growl. 'We'll work from both ends. With luck, we'll meet in the middle.'

CHAPTER THIRTY-SIX

I have all I need.

I have the Merc, which I can drive without fumbling around with a gear-stick; a car which is just about as unlike the Stag as you can get, and therefore not a mobile billboard for Harvey Russell, esq. I have a gun; Bill's gun, smuggled to him by his son, during the war years; a gun which—for 'sentimental' reasons—Bill has kept clean, oiled and in perfect working order; a genuine German Luger, complete with fully-loaded cartridge clip. I have an anger; a smouldering fury, the like of which I have not known for decades; a kill-or-be-killed urge to even the score ... to show these muscle-heavy bastards that Harvey Russell can give, just as readily as he can take.

I have Friday and, although Friday evening isn't *quite* the ball which Saturday evening can lay claim to, I know that (if past experience is any yardstick) Friday evening will find the yobs sniffing out the territory for Saturday evening's shindig.

Five gets you ten, Jim and his buddy-buddies will, at the very least, do a quick check-up on the night club.

I sip booze, slowly, and wait. I have chosen a shadowed alcove, from which I can watch the comings and goings. The Luger pulls my waistband a little out of line, but I keep my jacket buttoned and hope nobody notices the slight bulge.

They don't, and I am on my second whisky when the trio shoulder their way through the entrance.

I finish my drink, keep to the shadows and slip out to wait in the parked Merc.

I do not have to wait long. Within thirty minutes Jim, and his two cronies, are back on the street and the Merc's engine is already ticking as they pile into a waiting Escort.

I have luck riding alongside me, in the Merc. To follow another car is not easy, without being spotted—even I realise that—but the boyoes in the Escort keep to the busy streets, and the mid-evening traffic draws their attention and does much to hide the Merc. I keep well back from their tail—always with one, and sometimes two, vehicles between us—knowing that any unexpected turn can be dealt with via the Merc's thrust of acceleration. It is early darkness. A misty drizzle makes the wipers just necessary, and shines the road surface enough to reflect the lights of the streets and traffic. All these little things help ... they all add up to a margin of safety for which I am grateful.

The Escort brakes to a halt, at a corner shop in one of the less brightly lit streets. I drive the Merc past and, from my eye corner, see two of them cross the pavement to the door of the shop.

I turn into a side-street, switch off the engine, pocket the keys and return to the shop. I walk normally—not fast, not slow—and with my injured left hand in my jacket pocket. As I near the Escort I thumb the jacket button and rest my right hand on the grip of the Luger.

At the rear, nearside door of the Escort I stop, and turn. I keep my body as a shield as I ease the Luger from my waistband. Then, with my head above the roof of the car, I lean against the bodywork and thump the roof.

What happens is what *must* happen.

The door of the Escort is opened, and an annoyed face glares up at me. It is the face of the berk called John and, for that first moment, he doesn't recognise me.

'What the ...' he begins, then he stops.

He stops, because the snout of a Luger is within picking distance of his nose. From where he sits, that barrel must look as big as the mouth of the Mersey Tunnel.

'Don't faint, little man,' I say, gently. 'Don't scream ... or anything like that. Just do *exactly* as you're told and, with luck, you might see another sunrise.'

He stares up at me, and gasps, 'Christ, it's ...'

'That's who it is,' I agree. 'Alive, well and ready to collect his pound of flesh. Now—out of the car, creep ... and slowly. Any out-of-season jokes, and I part your hair, from inside.'

He swallows, nods and pushes himself, very carefully, from the upholstery. He is scared—very scared ... and with good and sufficient cause.

With his eyes on the Luger, he mutters, 'Is that—is it ...'

'It's real,' I assure him. 'And it fires real bullets. *And* it's loaded. Any more questions?'

I wave the Luger slightly, and he understands the sign language. He moves ahead of me, into the shop doorway.

'You get the first,' I promise him. 'You should know that ... in case you've a yen for posthumous medals.'

'I'll—I'll behave.'

'Good. You're not as dumb as you look, after all.' I jerk my head at the door. I say, 'How many inside?'

'T-two. We were together. The three of us. The other night—you—er—you met us, at the ...'

'Three of you arrived,' I agree. 'You stayed with the car. But how do I know other people weren't waiting?'

'We—er—we just wanna get some photographs. That's all. Then we were ...'

'Photographs?'

'Hard porn. Y'know ... wanking stuff. It's a newsagent's. We use the cellar as a store.'

'Is that a fact?'

'That's—that's where they'll be. In the cellar. Sorting it out.'

In the gloom of the doorway, I look hard at his face. I see fear. I think I see *enough* fear.

I jerk my head at the door, and ask, 'Is it locked?'

'Yer.'

'How do we unlock it?'

'I—er ...' He hesitates, until I line the Luger square on his navel, then he gabbles, 'I've—I've a key.'

I nod, and that is all the instruction he needs.

The shop is in darkness, but our eyes are, by this time, accustomed to the lack of light. He leads the way—less than twenty-four inches ahead of the Luger's snout—across the shop, behind the counter and into a back room.

The back room is not as dark as the shop. In one corner

there is an open door and, from this door, light filters up from the basement.

I tap the berk on the shoulder, with the barrel of the Luger, and he freezes. I motion him towards a battered armchair which stands alongside a cold, and ash-choked, hearth. He reads the signs aright, and obediently sits down in the chair.

It prevents undue noise. When I belt him across the skull with the Luger, he doesn't fall onto the carpet with an unwanted clatter. He merely folds forward in the chair, and goes to sleep.

The cellar steps are stone, therefore they don't creak. They are flanked, on each side, by unplastered, lime-washed brickwork. I work my way down them, gently—silently—and with the Luger held ready.

I am in the cellar, before anybody realises there is a visitor.

'The rules!' I snap. 'You've read the book. You know what's allowed.'

'Who the ...'

Jim drops a box-file as he spins to face me.

The one whose name I do not know, opens his mouth and gapes.

Jim says, 'Russell?' He drops his eyes to the gun, and sneers, 'You still kill-crazy?'

The naked bulb, hanging on its frayed flex, gives the tableau harsh light. We make the standard, stick-up group. One man with a gun. Two men, watching the gun—watching the gunman—and waiting for the next move, or the first opportunity.

I am a novice at this game, but the Luger gives a very heady feeling of power, and I've seen enough films and T.V. shows to know the correct sequence.

I wave the gun, and snap, 'The wall. Hands against the wall, and don't try anything.'

'Or?' asks Jim.

'This is a smash-up,' I warn. 'A return of favours. A hospital bed, or a slab ... personally, I don't give a damn which.'

I'm lying.

The unnamed one proves that I'm a liar.

As he turns for the wall he stoops and grabs for a broken stool. He makes the turn into a spin, straightens, and has the stool clear of the flagstones of the floor when he dies.

I do not remember squeezing the trigger. I do not remember aiming. All I know is that there is sudden noise. The noise of the explosion in the confines of the cellar. The short, sharp scream of the man, as the 9mm slug takes him in the face. The shout of mixed anger and warning, from the man called Jim. The clatter of the stool, as it flies and hits a stack of tins in a corner of the cellar.

Noise. Then, silence—the smell of cordite—the gentle swing of the electric light bulb, on its flex ... then, silence and a dead man.

I am trembling.

The hand holding the Luger is moist with sweat, and I can feel more sweat on my face and where the collar of my shirt meets my neck.

'Is he ...' I struggle to force the question past my constricted throat. 'Is he ...'

I don't end the question. Nor does it require an answer.

The man's face wears a blanket of blood. The back of his skull is like a smashed egg-shell, with the yolk of brains and the white of gore spilling and spreading on the stone floor.

Of course he's dead.

Jim's voice is soft and overflowing with hate, as he says, 'Now you've done it Russell. Now you've *really* done it.'

CHAPTER THIRTY-SEVEN

Don't ever let the psychologists tell you otherwise.

Self-preservation is the daddy of all impulses. It leaves the sex-urge cold. Anger, hunger, thirst ... they haven't a look in. When self-preservation claims the driving seat it takes over. Completely.

You kill a man. You shoot him to death. As of that moment, you stop thinking. Your brain flicks a switch and—just like that!—you turn animal. One part of your mind becomes a cold-blooded computer, working out the odds and ignoring the humanities. Self-preservation takes over.

I'd killed a man. Deliberately. Spontaneously. Inadvertently. Those were just words ... I'd killed a man. And, when you kill, civilised society demands vengeance. I (of all people) knew that. I was for the chop—I was for the big stick—I was banana-food ... unless I did certain things.

For example ... remove witnesses.

Logic ... you understand? The logic of pure self-preservation. To kill one, and leave two to tell the tale, was crazy. It wasn't even *trying*. And, with the no-topping law, what had I to lose? I'd still live. In captivity, if I was caught ... if not, in freedom. In captivity, for certain, if I left mouths which could talk.

You will appreciate that no sane man works it out like that; that no sane man positions the bricks of hard-headed logic in quite that manner. Instinct takes over. The pro's and the con's are weighed, one against the other, inside his mind while his body stands numb and helpless.

I know.

It happened!

Killing the man called Jim wasn't too difficult. His mind, too, raced towards the terminus and he tried one last, mad gamble. Why not? He knew it was a thousand-to-one chance . . . but he knew it was his *only* chance.

He tried to rush me.

The first bullet took him in the gut, punched him back against the wall and curled him into a sobbing ball. The second ended his anguish; through the centre of the chest —through the heart—at a range of less than twelve inches. I leaned forward, in order not to miss. I wanted to be merciful. I didn't want to inflict undue suffering.

Killing the man in the back room was more distasteful. To shoot an unconscious man, through the back of the neck, brings on nausea. It is not easy to hold the pistol steady. To squeeze the trigger. To watch the head jerk, rag-doll fashion, and see the blood spurt as one of the main arteries empties the body of life.

It is not a pleasant experience . . . but, when self-preservation drives, anything is possible.

The rest was easy.

I returned to the cellar, scattered the contents of the box-files—photographs showing fornication in all its crudity—added a score of untied bundles of old newspapers and magazines then, from the back room, added the contents of two packets of sugar and (of all things) all the firelighters from an unopened carton.

I worked one-handed, and awkwardly, with the Luger once more thrust into my waistband.

The thought struck me . . . that this was in the nature of an encore. That it had been done before—but not by me . . . although I'd been charged with the commission.

There's nothing new under the sun, and man learns his various tricks from other men.

In one corner of the cellar there was a gas meter. There was a movable spanner handy, so I disconnected the pipe, pulled it clear and snapped my lighter.

The flame curled and hissed, and made a furnace—or a crematorium—of the cellar. Almost before I started up the stairs, the sugar-sprinkled photographs and newspapers had caught and were starting to blaze.

I was in the Merc, and driving away, before controlled thought returned. Before realisation came back.

I'd claimed three lives, in exchange for two broken fingers.

And nothing—nothing on God's earth!—could connect me with the murdered men, whose bodies were roasting in the blaze.

Nice work, Harvey Russell. Nice work ... you are a very expensive man to cross.

CHAPTER THIRTY-EIGHT

You are also a murderer—a triple murderer—and Vi wonders what the hell is wrong.

Last night I couldn't sleep. Three times, I climbed from bed and wandered into the kitchen; the first time for milk, the second time for coffee and the third time— just before dawn—as a prelude to a return to the bathroom, for a shower and shave prior to giving the night up as lost and climbing into my clothes. I have smoked a full packet of cigarettes, during the time when I should have slept. I have prowled the house, like a caged cat, in my nervous agitation. I have rummaged every corner of my mind and my memory; seeking some link which might tie me to the killing and burning of the three men; standing in the imagined shoes of some investigating police officer, handling the case of triple-murder.

Some day—one day—I will sleep again. I will not be haunted by the thought of nightmares. I will forget (albeit temporarily) a man with a bullet-shattered face, a wounded man, shot like an ailing dog, and an unconscious man, blasted out of this world without even being aware of it.

Some day—one day—I will learn to live, and merely remember.

Vi says, 'God! You look rough.'

She has entered the breakfast room. She is wearing a padded nylon housecoat over her nightdress. Her feet are in sheepskin mules.

I grunt some sort of non-committal reply, and wish to hell she'd go back to bed.

'The fingers?' she asks.

'Eh?'

'Do they hurt, as much as that? Is that why you couldn't sleep?'

'Oh.' I raise my hand a few inches, and stare at it. 'The fingers.'

'Have you twisted them? Done some damage?'

'I have,' I say, softly and bitterly, 'done some damage. A considerable amount of damage.'

'You should see the doctor.'

'Damn the doctor.'

'Russ, if they're as painful as that, I think you really should ...'

'Damn the doctor. And damn *you*.'

She looks worried and uncertain. We have, during the time I've stayed here, built up a strange relationship. Not love. Certainly not respect. But, in some odd way, an inter-dependency. We need each other and, although that need might only be a temporary thing, its impermanence makes it no less vital. I treat her as I would treat a slut—as I would treat some cheap whore, from the street—and she responds with a fawning servitude which, at its worst, disgusts me. It disgusts me ... and yet it feeds my ego.

146

And, because it feeds my ego, the disgust expands until it also embraces myself.

She frowns her worry, and says, 'Look—if there's anything *I* can do.'

'Not a ...' I begin, then change my mind, and say, 'Yes ... there's one thing.'

'What?'

'If anybody asks—they won't ... but if they *do*.'

'Yes.'

'I was here last night. Yesterday evening. Since six ... until now.'

'Why? What have you ...'

'Nothing.'

'There must be *something*, if you ...'

'Nothing!' I shout. 'Now, for Christ's sake, if you really want to do something to help ... that's all. No bloody-fool questions. Just that. I was here—I've *been* here—since six yesterday, evening.'

And, what an amateur's way! I realise it, the moment it's out. The moment I see her eyes reflect suspicion and curiosity. She doesn't know what ... but she knows there's *something*. She knows that much. Damn it ... I've *told* her that much. Too much ... because anything, however little, is too much.

In God's name, how do men live with the crime of murder? How do they retain their sanity? How do they clear their mind of pictures ... pictures of blood, and death and moments which should never, *ever* have happened?

How do they stay silent? How do they act the part of normality? And, does genuine normality ever return? Is it possible? Is it possible to live long enough? Is it possible to bury that moment under the weight of enough years? To make it—not go away, because it'll never go away ... but to make it invisible?

The devil on your back ... do you ever *not* feel its crippling weight?

I'll know. One day, if I live long enough—if I stay sane long enough—I'll know the answer.

I mutter, 'I'm going out. For a walk. To walk it out of myself.'

'To walk what ...'

'The pain, if you like.' I give a quick smile which, I know, must look more like a monster's leer. 'That's it ... to walk the pain out of me. I'll be back. Sometime.'

CHAPTER THIRTY-NINE

I talk to him. I doubt if he hears me. I doubt if he understands—I doubt if he'll ever again understand ... but, nevertheless, I talk to him.

He lies there, in this tiny ward. Weeping silently, and cocooned in his own misery. Waxen-faced, motionless and with his right hand still resting, claw-like, on the coverlet.

I am wet, from the mid-March rain. I am tired, from having walked almost ten miles. I am a little crazy, from the thoughts which have churned and tumbled within my skull.

Nevertheless, I talk to him ... and, if he hears and understands, so be it.

I say, 'Old man, you've screwed things up. You've screwed things up ... but good. We had a firm ... remember? A good firm. One of the top firms in the country. We had this firm—you and I—and we were proud of it ... because it was *ours*. We'd built it. We swore we'd never do a scrap job. We swore we'd have standards ... and stick to those standards. The best, or nothing. No skimping. No corner-cutting. Nothing slipshod. Come hell, or high water, we were going to deal in class workmanship. In top-line materials.

'That was a dream, old man ... eh? That was *some* dream. Dreams come true. Sometimes. But this damn dream didn't. This damn dream turned sour on us. And —y'know what?—you helped it turn sour. You copped out. You chose the easy way. The sloppy way. The greedy way. You buggered everything up, old man, and you hadn't even the guts to tell me. Me! The berk who believed in you. The berk who couldn't swallow the truth ... that you were horse-trading. Wheeling and dealing. Taking this firm—our firm—*my* firm—and throwing the shit of corruption all over its name. That's what you did, Bill. To our firm. To the one man who called you "friend" ... and meant it. So, how far does friendship go ... eh? What price partnership? What price honesty? What price *anything*?

'You're dying, old man. I think you know it but, if you've any doubts, don't have ... you're dying. You're three-parts there, already. They'll bury you. Or burn you. And there'll be wreaths. A few empty words. Then, kaput. Finished. You'll weep no more, old man. Those eyes of yours ... they'll shed no more tears.

'Nor will any other eyes. No sorrow. No mourning. No heartbreak. But—who knows?—maybe that's what you want. Maybe you know what a broken crutch you've made of your life. Maybe you know what a cow you've married. That she spits at the very mention of your name. That she's open to any man ... including me. That, of late, I've taken your place in the shagging stakes. Maybe you know all these things, and don't give a damn.

'Is that it, old man? That you're disgusted with yourself? That you don't want to live with the louse you've turned yourself into? That, when you crucified the firm, you crucified yourself?

'I hope so. Damn you to hell, I hope so. I hope you've enough sense to understand, old man. Enough sense. Enough decency ... enough decency left, inside that chewed-up brain of yours.'

I stare at him, in silence, for all of two minutes.

Then, I say, 'Goodbye, old man. I won't come again. I doubt if anybody'll come again. You've turned me into a liar, a fool and, now, a murderer. You've worked it, Bill ... old man, old man. You've performed the miracle no-body else could perform. Live with it. For the rest of that tiny, miserable life you have left ... live with it!'

I doubt if he's heard me. I doubt if he's understood. But, I hope he has. I hope he now *knows*.

I leave him, wax-faced and motionless. Weeping, silently and with his claw-hand resting on the coverlet.

I could, so easily, feel pity for him.

But, why should I?

When the hell did he feel pity for *me*?

CHAPTER FORTY

And, who *is* suffering? Who *is* mad? Who *is* dead, short of the burial service? Bill Macks, or me?

It is Monday, and I haven't slept. Gumption insists that the human frame can take only so much. That, whatever the potential nightmares, there is a limit and, eventually, sleep must come. Three nights, without sleep ... and I still feel I can never sleep again. I feel I never *dare* sleep again.

I close my eyes and, every time, I pump bullets into men I don't even know. I kill them, then burn their bodies.

I collect newspapers and read, and re-read, accounts of

the infamy. What the police found. What the police suspect. What the police hope to achieve. And every word is a reminder ... that I have, inadvertently, committed the perfect crime.

The porn-shop angle ... the police lay great stress upon the photographs found in the cellar. A lead ... that's what they hint. That the miserable wretches whose disgusting contortions were captured on sensitised paper hold the vital clue to the killings. Those who can be traced are being 'interviewed' ... which means I have (equally inadvertently) created a beautiful red-herring.

It also means that people, somewhere, are having their souls exposed. That deep, gut-rotting misery is a spin-off to this crime of mine; that perversions are being prodded from their hiding places, and that shame is being splashed upon comparatively innocent folk who, from this day forth, will remain sullied ... and for no better reason than that I, a complete stranger, shot to death three men who were, to me, also complete strangers.

I created an earthquake, with those four trigger-pulls. I sent ripples and vibration away, and gone to hell.

Saturday and Sunday. I prowled the house. I prowled the grounds. I prowled the lanes, and the streets and roads of nearby towns and villages. I was incapable of relaxation.

And, all the time, my mind raced and spun like a runaway gyroscope. I ate little. I smoked constantly. I drank to excess, but couldn't become drunk.

And, on Sunday evening—for no good reason at all, other than I had to talk to *somebody* who was sane—I entered a telephone kiosk, looked up Kelly's home number and begged, like a frightened child, to be allowed to visit him.

He agreed ... reluctantly.

He was shocked at my appearance, but I wasn't there touting for sympathy. I wanted information; expert information upon matters—upon a profession, and a way of life—not too well-known to the general public. He fed me whisky—later, his wife fed me strong, sweet tea and paté sandwiches—and he answered my questions.

Later in the evening, he said, 'The enquiries. The firm ...'

'Smash it,' I said, tonelessly. 'Destroy it. It's a diseased thing ... that's all it's worth.'

'You're sure?' He looked puzzled. Uncertain.

'Those are my instructions,' I said. 'Tear the damn thing down, brick at a time. It doesn't exist any more. It's not what it claims to be—not what it was ... it doesn't deserve to live.'

'If—er—that's what you want.'

'That's what I *demand*.'

'I'll need your testimony,' he said, quietly.

'You'll get it. As much as you want, and when you want.'

'And then, the police ...'

'Hand the file to the police. Complete,' I said, harshly. 'The lot. Ready to prosecute. Keep a complete copy of the file at your office ... just in case.'

'Just in case what?'

I smiled. Tight-lipped and humourless.

I said, 'Roebuck can still pull strings. Documents can be misplaced. Evidence can disappear. If that happens ...'

'Yes?' He raised quizzical eyebrows.

I said, 'Kelly, you were an honest copper. They aren't *all*.'

'Oh!'

'They really *aren't* all,' I insisted.

I don't think he understood. I don't expect a man like Kelly—an ex-copper who, for almost half a century, has worked alongside men he admired and men he trusted—to ever completely understand.

No matter.

I know what I meant ... and, although Kelly will never

152

comprehend, his continuing ignorance is of no real importance.

And now it is Monday morning, and I have taken great pains with my toilet. I have bathed and soaked some of the weariness from my bones. I have shaved. I have dressed my hair with an almost finicky attention to detail. I have brushed my clothes, chosen my shirt and tie with care and made sure that my shoes are not mud-splashed.

I have (with some difficulty) worked a chamois leather glove over the fingers of my left hand; hiding the, by now, grimed strapping which holds the broken bones immobile.

Vi has watched me, with mounting interest—with mounting curiosity—and she can no longer keep her questions in check.

'Is it important?' she asks.

I nod.

'As important as all this?'

'It's important,' I sigh.

'To do with the firm? To do with Roebuck?'

'In a way. Indirectly.'

'Don't you ...' She frowns her shallow concern, then says, 'Don't you think you're making it unnecessarily rough on yourself?'

'No.'

'You can't change things. It's already gone too far.'

'Yes ... I know that.'

'So, why try?'

'I have a job to do,' I say quietly. 'I have a man to see.'

'A man?'

'A policeman.'

She eyes me with some small measure of contempt, as she lights her first cigarette of the day, then says, 'Y'know what you're doing? You're building your own cross.'

'It's possible.'

'You're playing at martyrs.'

'Maybe.'

'And nobody loves a martyr. They're weak. They're gutless. They just stand there, and let the world wipe their feet all over 'em. Nobody loves a martyr, Russ.'

'Ah, well.' From somewhere, I conjure up a lop-sided grin. 'I've done my share of feet-wiping. The role of door-mat might prove to be an interesting experience.'

She smokes her cigarette. She takes quick, jerky sucks at the corked-tip. She doesn't inhale. The smoke leaves her mouth at the moment it has passed her lips.

She says, 'They'll never be able to prove it.'

'I hope not.'

'Bill was a damn sight too careful for *that*.'

'Possibly ... but Bill's past caring.'

'He knew what he was doing.'

As I shrug the mac into position, across my shoulders, I say, 'The pity is, he didn't know what he was doing when he married you, sweetheart. His one big mistake ... that he didn't know what he was doing, then.'

CHAPTER FORTY-ONE

The same restaurant ... merely another meal.

It's odd—one of the coincidences which go to make up real life—that a thing should start and, more or less, end in similar circumstances. I am reminded of a remark I once heard made. About war ... that a war starts round a table, and ends round a table, and that the fighting and killing between those two table-conferences is, compara-tively speaking, superfluous. The sort of cocktail-party remark which sticks in your memory; strictly speaking, untrue ... but containing enough truth to encourage thought and argument.

We have, as before, just enjoyed a good meal. This time, at my expense. We are at the coffee-and-chat stage and, so far, we have talked of generalities. We have touched police work. We have mentioned the building trade, and the snags endemic to all major projects. We have aired the weather, prattled inanities, swopped likes, and dislikes relating to T.V., books and films, and we have even reminisced about our respective school-days.

So many words. All wasted. All meaningless.

It is time I steered the conversation around to face the target I have in mind.

I tap ash from the end of my cigarette, and murmur, 'The trial. You must have been disappointed.'

'The trial?' Perhaps he really doesn't quite understand. Or, perhaps the question is asked for some other reason.

'My trial,' I add.

'Oh ... that trial.'

'You must have been disappointed,' I repeat, gently.

'You win some, you lose some.' He pulls a mock-wry face. 'Our interest stops at the dock.'

'Theoretically.'

'It has to ... otherwise, we'd go mad.'

'Quite. But, having worked to build up a watertight case ...'

'There ain't no such thing.' He treats me to one of his quick, quirky smiles. 'It's the greatest lottery on earth. The best you can do is buy enough tickets.'

'Policing,' I observe, 'must be a strange profession.'

'Satisfying.'

'Man-hunting?'

'The biggest game of all,' he says, and there is a peculiar satisfaction in his tone.

'Ah, yes,' I agree. I sip my coffee, then add, 'For rankers, of course. But the P.B.I. Boring, surely. Frustrating.'

'Rank carries certain privileges,' he agrees.

'The big cases? Is that what you mean?'

'Yes ... the big ones. The *interesting* cases. Rank—rank such as mine, for example ... it sieves out the petty cases.'

'Yes. I suppose it does.'

'The lesser fry, we can leave to detective constables. Detective sergeants.'

'Of course ... I can see that.'

'And that leaves us free to concentrate our attention upon the *real* villains.'

'Are they around?' I ask, innocently.

'We have our share. Nothing like the Met, of course. They have scores. We have a mere handful. But we have our share of hard cases. Enough to keep us amused.'

'It would seem,' I observe, 'that there's a distinct pecking-order. Am I right?'

'Yes ... you could put it that way. With the villains ... and with the police. It wouldn't do—say—for a detective constable to go after one of the big-time criminals. That needs a superior officer.'

'Interesting,' I murmur.

'But obvious ... surely?'

CHAPTER FORTY-TWO

I am gradually being made aware of this man's inordinate pride in his rank. He uses a phrase. 'Superior officer'. What he really means is *'senior* officer' ... but there is an unconscious arrogance which insists that he uses the incorrect terminology.

I have ordered a carafe of wine. Vintage, smooth and deceptive. I chose it carefully. It is liquid silk to the palate. but liquid dynamite to the inhibition.

We savour this drink, smoke our cigarettes and talk.

The restaurant gradually empties, except for ourselves, two other groups of conversing men at distant tables and a handful of hovering waiters.

He has a strong head for booze, but I have a thick edge on him. For three days, now, I have been trying to drink myself into a state of stupefied forgetfulness, and I am still stone-cold sober.

One more bottle of wine isn't going to make any difference.

CHAPTER FORTY-THREE

'I'm curious,' I say, off-handedly.

'What about?'

'The rank. You ... being a chief inspector.'

'It's a good rank,' he protests, mildly. 'It's a pretty important rank.'

'Ah, yes,' I hedge, 'but—y'know ...'

'No. What?'

He nibbles at the ground-bait very nicely. Eagerly. Greedily. A game fish who, smart though he may be, is not as smart as he thinks he is ... and who, if played with sufficient skill, can be out-smarted.

I say, 'A doctorate. A degree, the size you hold. Surely to God, you should be a superintendent—a chief superintendent ... at least that.'

'Maybe,' he mutters, and takes a fair-sized swig of wine.

'Why not?' I ask, guilelessly. 'Are they all idiots in the Police Service? Don't they appreciate what a Ph.D. stands for?'

He moves his shoulders, and a look of peeved anger touches his expression.

'So, why not?' I press.

'Like all things,' he growls. 'Like all jobs. Your face fits ... or it doesn't fit.'

'Surely not?'

'You'd be surprised.'

'I *am* surprised,' I murmur ... and augment the remark with a look of mild incredulity.

'They're there,' he assures me, solemnly. 'The dim bulbs. The thick bastards. They're still in the bull's-eye-lantern-and-big-stick era ... and they won't be damn-well *told*.'

'It must be frustrating,' I sympathise.

'Sometimes.' Then, he opens his heart a little wider, and adds, 'Often.'

'So-o ... slow promotion?'

He nods, swirls the wine in his glass, and murmurs, 'Funereal.'

There is a silence. Of sympathy, perhaps. Or, perhaps, of commiseration. Whatever ... of something.

Then, I say, 'Good job you're not married.'

'Eh?'

He looks up, from staring at the rim of his glass.

'Married,' I repeat. 'Women get uptight about these things.'

'Ye-es. I suppose they do.'

'Especially wives.'

'I suppose so.'

'Wives are ambitious,' I continue. 'Sometimes—y'know ... *too* ambitious.'

'You've mentioned it.'

'Have I?' I look surprised. Slightly befuddled.

'On the day you were acquitted.'

'Oh!'

There is another lamination of silence in this structure of talk which I am carefully building. Silence, in which I grope, with infinite caution, for the next step. Silence, in which Crawford sips his wine, smokes his cigarette and, for the moment, sits alone with his thoughts.

Then, as if to break the boredom of silence, I murmur, 'Any chance?'

'Eh? What of?' He blinks himself back to part-concentration.

'Marriage? Y'know ... have you any plans along those lines?'

'Good Lord, no. No ... not in a million years.'

The negative answer to my question is just a *leetle* over-emphasised.

I smile, and say, 'That's a hell of a long time.'

'What?'

'A million years.'

'Ah, could be.' A wry grin flickers across his face, and he repeats, 'Could be.'

'No girl-friends?' I ask.

'Uhu. Occasionally.'

'But—y'know ... nothing serious?'

'What's "serious"?' he counters, and there is a hint of bitterness in his tone. Wine-induced bitterness.

'Permanent,' I say.

He hesitates, then mutters, 'She didn't appreciate it.'

'You?'

'Eh?' The blink and the stare are pointers to the state of his concentration.

'Y'mean she didn't appreciate *you*?' I amplify.

'No ... that she didn't.'

'A fool,' I sigh.

'A silly bitch. I'm better without her.'

'That sort,' I agree. I sip my wine, smoke another fraction of an inch of my cigarette, then ask, 'How long's that since?'

'Eh?'

'Since she walked out? Or did you walk out on her?'

'She went,' he says, flatly. 'Good riddance.'

'What was she?' I ask.

159

'Eh?'

'A policewoman? I imagine some of the ...'

'No. A nurse.'

'Oh!' My raised eyebrows invite further details.

'She just blew. Some weeks back—a couple, or three, months ago ... she just up, and went. Left the hospital. Left everything. Just up, and went ... just like that.'

'And, since then, nothing?'

'After that?' His lip curls, and he repeats, 'After *that*?'

CHAPTER FORTY-FOUR

Odd ...

It requires a conscious effort to remember that I'm a triple-murderer. A few hours ago, I couldn't *forget*. The knowledge was there, like a brand-mark in the middle of my forehead. Three men, shot to death ... and my finger had been on the trigger.

Now ...

This intricate saraband of words demands concentration. The wrong phrase—the wrong emphasis—and the tempo will be broken. The tune will be lost. The truth will never be coaxed from its hiding place.

It is, therefore, necessary that I ignore everything—*everything!*—other than the slow weave and movement of this conversation.

CHAPTER FORTY-FIVE

'You're a nice bloke,' I say. Then, with a smile, I add, 'For a policeman.'

He returns the smile.

'I mean—y'know ...' I move my head. 'Coming to see me, after the beat-up.'

I glance at my gloved hand.

'What else?' He helps himself to another cigarette, from the open packet on the table. 'We have certain—er ... "links".'

'A murder,' I agree.

'I almost nailed you,' he remarks, wrily.

'Nearly.'

'If it hadn't been for that bloody jury.'

'But—y'know ... no hard feelings.'

'None at all,' he murmurs.

I say, 'And—at least—I gave you the confession you wanted.'

He looks at me, and gives a single nod. His eyes are slightly glassy—very slightly ... but glassy. The wine is working at his brain.

'Not that you really believed me,' I remark.

'Why not?'

'Oh ... come *on*!'

'We-ell, maybe not.' There is a quick, shamefaced grin. 'But it was a good try. I *nearly* nailed you.' His forehead furrows, and he adds, 'Anyway ... why *did* you confess to a murder you didn't commit?'

'Swank, I suppose. We all like being clever. I wanted you to think I'd got away with something.'

He nods, sagely.

'Which,' I say, 'makes your visit to the hospital an even nicer gesture.'

'Nothing. Nothing at all.'

'And, on a Sunday, too.'

'Sunday—any day—they're all the same to coppers.'

'Oh! I thought you usually took the weekends off.'

'We-ell—yea ... sometimes.' He pauses, then admits, 'Often, I suppose. One of the perks of the rank.'

'Out of your own police district, too,' I observe, off-handedly.

'Not too far. Not a day's march away.'

'No—but, y'know ... not on your own doorstep.'

'Forget it,' he says, magnanimously. 'If ever *I'm* horizontal, you can return the compliment.'

I am reminded of brickwork. Fancy, out-of-the-ordinary brickwork, which only a skilled craftsman would attempt. Patterned brickwork, where one wrongly placed brick would weaken the whole structure.

And, if the words are the bricks, the silences are the carefully mixed mortar which holds them in place.

It is time for a little more mortar. A little more silence.

This time, he breaks the silence, with, 'That corruption thing you mentioned. I've ...'

'Forget it.'

'You want me to?'

'As a favour.'

'Of course.'

'It was,' I say, 'a mistake. One of those things ... actually, one of *two* things. Not connected.'

He puts on a wise expression, and says, 'I thought you were jumping the gun.'

'Understandably,' I argue, mildly.

'Oh, yes ... naturally.'

'I mean—I'm framed for a murder I didn't commit, almost immediately after I stumbled across some back-door palm-greasing. The two things seemed to go together. But, they didn't.'

'Which leaves Roebuck in the clear?'

'As far as the murder's concerned,' I admit.

He hesitates, draws on the cigarette, moistens his lips with more wine, then says, 'Can you take advice, Russell?'

'If it's good.'

'The best.'

'Okay ... if it's that good, I'd be a fool not to take it.'

'Leave well alone, old son.'

'Well?'

'The dropsy side of things. It happens all the time.'

'I can believe you.'

'And, it's hell's own job to prove.'

'That, I'm prepared to believe.'

'So,' he says, 'leave well alone. Don't tangle with a man like Roebuck. He knows too many "right" people.'

'If you say so,' I agree, heavily. Then, I continue, 'You've enough on your plate, as it is.'

'Uhu. Every day. The crime load gets heavier by the hour.'

'And now this murder,' I murmur.

'Eh? Which murder?'

'My wife. The murder of my wife. I didn't kill her. *Somebody* did. You're back at square one ... with all that work wasted.'

CHAPTER FORTY-SIX

So far ...

I must now let the bricks settle into place, and allow the mortar to harden a little. I estimate that I have reached the crucial weight-ratio; that this flimsy house-that-Jack-built is likely to rock, then fall, if any more load is added to the carefully balanced walls I have already erected.

I make a suggestion. Off-handedly, and giving the impression that I couldn't care less whether, or not, he agrees with the idea.

I suggest that we drive out to Yew Cottage. To show him what a magnificent job the workmen have performed, in restoring it to its former beauty. To bring back nostalgia ... memories of a battle won, and a battle lost. He agrees, without question. He makes a smiling remark about 'the criminal always returning to the scene of his crime', but I allow the remark to pass me, without comment.

We finish what is left of the wine, leave the restaurant and climb into the Merc.

We set off for Yew Cottage ... and three bottles of Drambuie. The grain, to mix with the grape; the gassing mixture which, with luck, will tap the wedge into position, ready for hammer-blows which (again, with luck) will widen the flaws and crack this case from top to bottom.

We drive in the Merc.

Crawford is a good passenger. He hands full responsibility for the driving of the car, to me. He refrains from offering advice. At junctions he restrains himself, and doesn't come the 'all-clear-at-this-side' chat which all drivers dislike, and all good drivers ignore.

Indeed, he dozes. He relaxes in the front passenger seat, closes his eyes and cat-naps a good fifty-per-cent of the way.

We arrive, I park the car, unlock the front door and lead Crawford into the downstairs room. It is a fine room; the best room my money can buy. The men have repaired it, and it has been thoroughly cleaned. I defy anybody to spot where the damage has been. The floor has a new wall-to-wall carpet. The smoke-blackened paintwork has been removed. The whole room has been re-decorated. Curtains, furniture and rugs have all been replaced.

It is, once more, my 'home'.

'Very affluent,' murmurs Crawford.

'It proves something.'

'What?'

'A certain arithmetical progression. That hard work, and honesty, can bring money ... and, money can bring this.' I wave a hand to a deep armchair, and add, 'Try that one for size, friend. Yours will be the first backside it's ever held.'

As he sits, he says, 'Fine. Shouldn't we break a bottle of champagne ... or something?'

'Or something,' I agree. 'Relax. I'll find a christening bottle.'

In less than five minutes, we are sprawling in twin armchairs, slopping Drambuie down our throats.

'Nice drink,' he remarks.

'I like it.'

'Very tasty. Not too strong.'

I say, 'Quite.'

Drambuie. The nectar of the Gods. Like the wine we drank, earlier, it creeps up on you; as innocent-tasting as liquid velvet—as soothing as a warm breeze, from the sea ... but, with a delayed kick, like nothing on earth.

The central heating is working fine, nevertheless, I flick on all three bars of the electric fire. The room gradually becomes warmer—even oppressive—and, as I watch his face for signs, I see the eyelids lower, fractionally, before he blinks them wide in a sudden return to concentration. I hear his speech; not yet blurred—not yet confused—but, if not mouthed with an unnatural deliberation, a little fuzzy at the edges.

He is not yet drunk—nor, come to that, do I want him drunk ... he is merely 'happy'.

CHAPTER FORTY-SEVEN

'That was some trial,' I muse. 'An experience I wouldn't like to live through again.'

'You get used.'

'That,' I say, with some solemnity, 'I very much doubt.'

'Believe me. There isn't a Crown Sitting—or, before that, a Quarter Sessions or an Assize ... I was at 'em all.'

'Ah, yes. But not charged.'

'No—of course not ... not *that*.'

'And innocent, with it.'

'If you *were* innocent.'

'Crawford ... you know that damn well.'

'Probably.' In a dreamy voice, he continues, 'Murder ... I wonder why the book-writers pretend it's so hard to prove. It's snip-easy. If you play your cards right.'

'Really?'

I am easing my way across wafer-thin ice. Over-anxiety will drive him back into his hole. Not enough curiosity might give him the impression that I'm not interested. I take what has been given to me, make the most of it, and bluff spades for all I'm worth. I sip the liqueur and allow my face to act out an expression which (I hope) conveys slight, but not overwhelming, interest, with a touch of boredom and a thin thread of disbelief.

He glares irritation, and says, 'You don't believe me ... do you?'

'Did I say that?'

'Your whole expression. Your whole attitude.'

'I'm sorry.' I smile a friendly smile. 'But—y'know ... it *is* the big crime. And British justice, being what it is ...'

'Ah, long live British justice,' he interrupts, and the interruption is heavy with bitterness and contempt. 'The old whore in a nightdress, holding aloft her "scales of justice". "Scales of justice", my arse, friend. They're a couple of begging bowls, and whoever tips one against the other wins ... hands down.'

'You sound disillusioned,' I murmur, encouragingly.

'Disillusioned! Years ago, mate ... *years* ago.' He throws some whisky down his throat, places the glass onto a side-table, leans forward in the chair, rests one elbow on his leg, just above his knee and uses a stiffened forefinger to poke his arguments across at me. He says, 'All right ... take you. You were charged with knocking Lissa. So far, so good. You *didn't* ... but that's beside the point. I'd enough evidence. More than enough. Motive. Means. Opportunity. The Holy Trinity, as far as a successful prosecution's concerned. Your gun. Your place ... this place. No witnesses. You hate the sight of her ... and wouldn't say otherwise. Russell, you were over the biggest barrel ever built. But you got away with it. D'you know why?'

He's going to tell me, so I don't answer. Instead, I wait.

'Circumstantial evidence,' he sneers. 'That's all. The courts don't like it. Give 'em a knife stuck in somebody's guts—some poor bitch who's had all she can take from a louse of a husband, and who rams the carver home, then runs to the nearest cop to tell him what she's done ... give 'em *that*, and they're happy. Nothing "circumstantial" ... see? They're on firm ground. But, with you, it was *all* circumstantial. Dabs, on the gun ... but, it was your blasted gun, so who else's fingerprints? Your cottage ... but it *is* your cottage, so why *shouldn't* you be there? Nobody saw you arrive ... so, who came first, you or her? Ballistics evidence—all right ... the shots came from your rifle but, the way the court argues, does that prove you pulled the trigger?

'A whole bundle of "possibilities'—even "probabilities" —and it's not enough. Why? Because they're all circumstantial evidence. Nothing concrete. No eye-witnesses ... as if anybody's likely to commit premeditated murder in front of a bloody audience.'

'It must be frustrating,' I murmur, sympathetically.

'Frustrating!' He almost spits. I have the distinct impression that, were it not for the brand-new carpet, he actually *would* have spit out his disgust. Instead, he snarls, 'This job brings it home to you, Russell. That "justice" we're so bloody proud of. I've seen villains ... villains who should have been strangled at birth. I've seen judges ... judges who couldn't add up to five, without using their fingers and thumb. And, as for *juries*! God help all policemen when they're pushing the truth down the throats of a jury ... it can't be done.'

'Still ...' I begin.

He interrupts, and continues, 'Look, Russell, you're not unique. Everybody gets away with everything, these days. It's the way of things. Like murder. Sod the corpse— bugger the murderer—if it's circumstantial evidence, it's chalked up as one more bad debt. Undetected. The courts want eye-witnesses, confessions and guilty pleas ... otherwise, they won't play ball.'

'Ah, but *I* didn't get away with anything,' I remind him, in a soft, flat voice.

'Eh?'

'I didn't murder Lissa.'

'No ... so you say.'

'And, so you believe ... you remarked upon that belief a few minutes ago.'

'Did I?' He frowns his concentration.

'I *didn't* knock Lissa—your exact words.'

'We-ell ... maybe not.'

CHAPTER FORTY-EIGHT

Stay with me, luck. Stay with me, madam ... don't desert me, at this late stage. I need you, as never before. I need your guile, your cunning, your subterfuge. I need a knavery which I lack. A duplicity which is against my nature. A deception which is not part of my make-up.

This policeman—this detective chief inspector—from whom I must trick the truth, is human. He *must* be human. Which means he must be capable of making mistakes. Foolish mistakes which, if used wisely, can entice him into the trap I have in mind.

I inject slight petulance into my tone, as I ask, 'Then, why the devil aren't you out looking for him?'

'Eh? Who?'

'The man who killed Lissa.'

'We are. Of course we are. We don't let murderers get ...'

'Not as I see it,' I interrupt.

'You're a bit biased, old man.'

'I'm entitled to be a bit biased ... "old man",' I come back at him, in a half-snarl.

'You've had a rough passage. You're bound to be sore about the whole thing.'

'I have,' I say, coldly, 'been at the receiving end of the biggest load of crap ever thought up by civilised man. I have been made to stand in a Crown Court, listening to a long drawn-out pack of lies, and each lie a nail in my own coffin. Biased! Too damn right, I'm biased.'

My outburst shakes him a little. He stares at me, with slightly out-of-focus eyes and, in a voice tinged with sad-

ness,' he says, 'Russell, old man. We're human. The police
—y'know ... we're only human. We make mistakes, sometimes. Not often ... but sometimes.'

'You knew I was innocent,' I accuse him ... and, now,
it's out in the open. 'You knew damn well I was innocent.
Even before you charged me.'

'Naw—naw ... that's not fair. If we'd even thought ...'

'You've already admitted it. Not five minutes ago. That
I didn't kill Lissa. Your exact words ... think back. And—
let me impress upon you—that decision hasn't just arrived,
Recorded Delivery, like a bolt of lightning. It's been there
a long time. It was there, long before you charged me ...
but it didn't *stop* you from charging me.'

'We deal in facts, old man. Facts ... that's all.' He blinks,
owlishly. 'I'm sorry, but personal opinions don't count.'

'No?' I sneer.

'How else? How otherwise?'

The constriction of the glove is making the broken
fingers of my left hand ache a little. I massage them,
gently, as I say, 'All that bull about circumstantial evidence, Crawford. Other evidence was available ... but you
either ignored it, or soft-pedalled it. You weren't out for
justice—"old man" ... you were going flat-out for a
conviction.'

'That's a nasty accusation, Russell,' he says, in what
would, without the recent intake of liquor, have been a
hard and warning tone. Instead, it comes out a boozed-up
berk's very empty threat.

I top his glass to the brim, and he does nothing to dis-
courage me.

Then, I say, 'Let's start with the moment you entered
this place—this cottage—let's check on the scene. A dead
woman, on the floor ... right?'

He nods.

'Blazing. Petrol, paraffin thrown over her, and she was
burning?'

'She was dead. She was burning,' he agrees.

'And there is poor little me. Harvey Russell ... the patsy to end all patsies. Standing there, like a pile of loose change. Doing what? Doing exactly what, "old man"? Doing exactly *what*?'

'You had the gun in your hand.'

'At hip-level ... right?'

He nods.

'Cowboy-and-Indian fashion?'

'At hip-level. Pointing it at the corpse.'

'The blazing corpse?'

'You know damn well. Yes. Pointing it at the burning body ... and with your finger on the trigger.'

'Now, why,' I ask, smoothly, 'should I be doing that?'

'If you'd killed her ...'

'If I'd killed her, I wouldn't be pointing the bloody gun at her.'

'Making sure. Unless you'd ...'

'I'd sloshed petrol—paraffin—all over her. That, in itself, would have been a two-handed job. I'd struck a match ... or something. Play the cards whichever way you like, Crawford, I'd have had to put down the gun. I'd have checked she was dead. So why—for Christ's sake, *why*—should I pick up the gun, again and point it at an already dead woman?'

He shakes his head, as if to jerk some degree of sobriety back to his befuddled brain.

He mutters, 'I—er—I think I'll have to go, now. Thanks for the meal, and the ...'

'I think you'll stay,' I snap. 'There are certain things—certain moments of truth—in every man's life. This is one of yours ... and you're not going to miss it.'

171

CHAPTER FORTY-NINE

And mine ...

It is a moment of truth in my life, too. Equal to—possibly even greater than—Crawford's. To know that I have him. To know that he is in the trap, and that, short of a complete dog's dinner, on my part, the door of the trap must slam closed and hold him prisoner.

I feel elation (who wouldn't?) but, at the same time, I feel a growing, and utterly illogical, fear. What if I haven't the skill? What if I lack the cunning? What if I ask the wrong question? ... or if he isn't quite drunk enough? ... or (even) if his half-drunkenness is a deliberate act, calculated to egg me on, prior to slapping me down into nothingness.

And (who knows?) maybe the wine is befuddling *my* brain, too.

I choose my words, carefully. I proceed with extreme caution. I keep my fingers tightly crossed.

I say, 'That fire—the burning of the body—it can't have helped the medic.'

'Eh? How so?'

'Time of death,' I say, quietly. 'Body temperature. I know little about those things ...'

'Who does?'

'... but—as I understand these things—estimated time of death has a whale of a lot to do with body temperature. The temperature of the air surrounding a body. The rate of cooling ... am I right?'

'Yes, you're right.' He squints his concentration and, visibly, tries to jump ahead of my train of thought.

172

I say, 'Slosh petrol over a body—especially a fully-clothed body—strike a match, and calculations go slightly askew ... wouldn't you say?'

'It—er—it makes it difficult,' he admits, reluctantly.

'It makes it damn near impossible,' I snap.

'Difficult,' he insists, doggedly.

'All right—I'll concede the point ... "difficult".'

I feed him more Drambuie. He accepts it, without protest. He is almost beyond the point of fighting back.

I say, 'Which means—in effect—that neither you, the medics, nor Father Christmas himself can say, with any degree of real certainty, when the murder was committed. One hour, two hours, three hours ... and all stations, south to Hell. Shoot her. Sprinkle inflammable liquid onto her clothes ... and she *was* a damn sight more burned than the rest of the room suggests she should have been. Keep the home fires burning, and everything's neat and tidy. Correction ... everything's screwed up to hell and beyond. Time of death becomes little more than a ticket drawn at a Sunday School raffle. Agreed?'

'And, if you're right?' he mutters. '*Supposing* you're right ... how do you prove it?'

'I dunno,' I admit.

'So-o, you're talking cock, Russell. You're talking un-diluted cock.'

'You *hope*.'

'Look!' He swigs the juice down in a single gulp, decides to be nasty, and snarls, 'Just what sort of accusations are you making, Russell? Just what sort of ...'

'A woman was killed,' I rap. 'I didn't kill her. For my own peace of mind, I want to know who *did*. And why. I want to know why I was framed.' I insert the exact size of pause, then add, 'And, bastard, I want to know why you had a hand in framing me.'

'You're crazy!'

'Sane ... for the first time in years.'

'I'm not going to sit here, and listen ...'

'Your choice, Crawford. Me, or a Home Office Enquiry.
Don't rush to a decision. Take your time—weigh the odds
... then, let me know.'

What a decision! Talk about 'Where will you have it—
the belly, or the back?' That is the brand of choice he
has ... and he knows it. Over the meal, here in the cottage,
I have weighed this sweet bastard up. I have met his type
before. Often ... but never as absolute as this one. And
I'm right. Too damn right I'm right. The booze, the
conviviality and his own supreme self-assurance have
kicked the ground from under him. He is dancing around
in mid-air, feeling for a foothold which doesn't exist.

I pour myself some more booze, pass the half-empty
bottle to the table alongside his chair. One part of my
mind sympathises with him; a proud man, a self-sufficient
man—a man very much like myself ... and he's nailed,
very firmly, to some red-hot floorboards ... he needs something to counteract the pain.

CHAPTER FIFTY

Five, never-ending minutes.

It can be a short time, it can be a long time but, for
Crawford, it is almost forever. I give him the time. I
would, willingly, give him *fifty* minutes—and fifty-times-
fifty minutes—if only in order that he examine the various
false escape routes, and recognise them for what they are
... false.

I watch the expressions move across his face, like clouds
across a darkening sky. Anger. Frustration. Bitterness.
Disgust. But, not once—not for a fraction of a second—

self-pity ... and, for that I admire him.

He sips Drambuie ... sipping it, gently, this time, as if giving his hands work to do while he ponders upon my ultimatum. Then, after five minutes of thoughtful silence, he speaks. He speaks, if not as a friend, as an honourable enemy. He speaks as an equal and, in return, I grant him the right of equality.

He says, 'How much do you know? How much is guess-work?'

'Enough to make the guesswork *good* guesswork.'

'That's an easy claim to make,' he murmurs.

'You're not popular, Crawford,' I remind him. I'm not here to pull punches; I'm here to kayo him—swiftly, or slowly ... but with absolute certainty. I say, 'Your fellow-coppers don't vote you the man-of-the-year.'

'It means little.'

'It means you're not conscientious. You do as much work as you must ... but no more.'

'Assuming that to be a fact. What of it?'

'A beat-up?' I mock, gently. 'A going-over. It happens every night. In every police district. A mugging. A rolling. A minor hospital case. And not even in your police area ... but you trotted along to commiserate. *And* on a Sunday. You don't work, Sundays, Crawford. There's a detective sergeant ready and eager to pop that snippet of information into the pot. Saturdays—Sundays—he carries you ... he doesn't know where the hell you get to. *But you knew.* You knew all about the beat-up, and you came along. Just to make sure. To make quite sure I didn't know any of the bully-boys. The tough babies who'd smashed me around, because I was asking questions just a *leetle* bit too near the bone. About the rigmarole necessary to get somebody killed. They passed the word on to you. They dusted me around—on your orders ... then you came along to check that my description wasn't worth a parson's fart. Okay?' I smile at him, without animosity. 'Is the score totting up, would you say?'

He returns the smile, and says, 'You're a long way from the jackpot, Russell. Some of it you could prove ... maybe. Most of it's my word against yours.'

'My word against yours,' I muse. 'Your word against mine. So-o ... let's talk about motor cars. Let's talk about guns. Lissa's car was parked outside. Lissa had a key to the cottage ... the *only* key, other than my own. Lissa opened that door, friend. She *had* to. The question arises ... why? She didn't like this place. She *never* liked it. The bright lights—the big shops—the pavement jungle ... that's what *she* liked. So, why come out here? To see me? ... not on your sweet life, friend. We've hated each other's guts for years. So-o—not to see me ... but because *I* was going to be here. There's a difference, Crawford. One hell of a difference.

'There's also been a certain presumption. Y'know ... one of those unimportant little facts, so obvious as not to need mentioning. *That Lissa wasn't alone.* Everybody's taken it for granted, haven't they? That the poor little darling drove here, all by herself, in her beautiful new Toledo ... and why, for Christ's sake? Not to see me, Crawford. That, above all else ... not to see me. So-o— *not* alone ... and, when she'd let herself, and whoever was with her, into the cottage, she fished the gun from the back of the wardrobe. *She* took it out. *She* knew it was there. Y'know, Crawford, old son, these itsy-bitsy questions, and their itsy-bitsy answers tend to alter the complexion of this whole, magnificent shunt-up ... don't you think?'

'*You* think ... obviously,' counters Crawford with a smile. 'I'm merely interested in *what* you think.'

'For the moment.' I match smile for smile.

'For the moment,' he agrees.

I am suddenly aware that he is sober. Stone-cold sober, and deadly dangerous. Maybe the drunk act was just that

... an act. On the other hand, maybe the approach of real danger had blown the fumes away, and cleared his mind.

'I think,' I say, slowly, 'that I've been chasing the wasp, and ignoring the honey. It happens, sometimes. Conjurers use the same sweet trick. Make the right hand look busy, while the left hand's doing all the work. They do it deliberately ... I've been falling for the same trick, accidentally.'

'Roebuck?' He actually chuckles—quietly, but genuinely —as he asks the question.

I say, 'Uhu ... Alderman Maurice Roebuck. The big fixer. The horse-trader. He had damn-all to do with the murder. He knew my wife. He bought her the Triumph. After that ... sweet F.A. His bad luck was that the Triumph was at the murder scene. People jumped to conclusions.'

'*You* jumped to conclusions,' Crawford corrects me.

'The silver lining,' I muse, sombrely.

'What's that?'

'Bill Macks didn't frame me.' I stare into Crawford's face. 'That I couldn't have stomached. Weakness ... okay. The fast buck ... maybe it is necessary, these days. But whatever else—he didn't stand me up, falsely charged with murder..'

'Does it follow?' taunts Crawford.

'No Roebuck. No Bill Macks. It follows,' I growl.

'So, now what? "Hearts and Flowers"?'

'No,' I say, harshly, 'now the little matter of a hoax call. A *suspected* shopbreaking. Get it, Mr Detective Chief Inspector Crawford. Two indefinites. A hoax. And a "maybe". And you—the big white chief, with a detective sergeant to hold your lily-white hand—rush off into the wide blue yonder ... chasing what? Not even ghosts. Not even a positive crime. And you, the killer-diller of this area's C.I.D. drop everything and go slightly haywire. You do something ... *completely out of character*.' I pause, then say, 'I wonder why?'

'You're ...' He swallows and, for the first time, the voice comes from a drying throat. 'You're calling the shots, Russell. *You* tell *me*.'

'We-ell, now ...' I let him sweat a little, while I light a cigarette, and I feel foolish pride in the fact that my hand shows no sign of tremble. I blow smoke, then I say, ' "Suspected" ... especially when it's a hoax call. You can take as long as you like. Or, as short as you like. Five minutes. Two hours. You name it ... you're the boss. It cuts out all this split-second, French farce garbage the clever-clever alibi-workers sweat cobs building up. You're already out on a job. You're available ... and can stay available, just as long as the fancy takes you. More than that, you've a dinger of a witness. A detective sergeant, who doesn't like you overmuch ... who certainly wouldn't lie for you. Sweet work, Crawford. I could very easily admire you for it.'

'For—for what?' he whispers.

'For the murder, here—at Yew Cottage—on Twelfth Night ... what the hell else?'

'How the devil could I ...'

'You fixed it, friend. You organised the killers. Lissa opened the door for 'em. She showed 'em where the gun was. They used it ... then they kept the corpse nice and warm, pending my arrival ... at which point they moved out, the back way, and left me to pick up the pieces.'

He says, 'Agatha Christie would be green with envy.'

It is meant to be sarcasm ... but it is *not* sarcasm. It is bluff. One last throw of the dice; a double-or-quits throw ... with the greatest stake in the world at risk.

I toss questions at him, in quick succession.

He tries to answer them. He makes a fine attempt to answer them—being what he is, being who he is, he *must* make a fine attempt ... but they are unanswerable.

'Why should I phone the police?' I ask, softly.

'A double-bluff.'

'Why use my own gun?'

178

'Why not? It's handy ... *was* handy.'

'Guns are easy to come by, Crawford.'

'Tell me, sometime. It's information I could use.'

'Why leave my fingerprints all over everything?'

'Why not? It's your cottage.'

'And Lissa's fingerprints?'

'Again—why not? She was here.'

'Why not make a good job? Burn the damn place down to its foundations? ... corpse, and all?'

'People panic. It happens all the time.'

'Why not take her outside? Shoot her in the open?'

'You don't have cat's eyes, Russell. You needed light.'

'Why try to destroy the corpse?'

'You tried. You tried very hard.'

'Okay—let's say I tried very hard ... why leave her car outside?'

'People make foolish mistakes. That's why they come unstuck.'

'Okay—why kill her, in the first place?'

'That's a question only you can answer.'

'I hated her guts.'

'That's what *you* say.'

'Why *shouldn't* I hate her guts?'

'You tell me.'

'That damn car—Roebuck's present to her ... she worked for it.'

'That's what *you* say.'

I am getting through to him, at last. The voice is harsh and ugly. The expression is set in a barely concealed mask of hatred. The eyes are narrowed and overflowing with fury.

'She worked for it,' I repeat, gently. 'The only way she knew how. On her back.'

'You can't prove that.'

'I wouldn't waste the energy. The sun rises, tomorrow

morning. I can't prove that, either ... until dawn breaks. But I *know*.'

'She was a good woman,' he croaks.

'Did she tell you that?' I taunt.

'No! I make my own assessments.'

'Of course ... like you assessed me as a murderer.'

'I presented a case. Facts, from which the jury could reach a decision.'

I snap, 'You presented *some* facts. Slanted facts. Facts wrapped up in moonshine. Your own particular brand of moonshine. You almost pulled it, Crawford. Almost! That's why you hared down into the cell area. That's why you pulled the buddy-buddy gag. To see whether I'd guessed anything. Guessed a little too much, maybe. You were scared, friend.' I stare at him, coldly, through the rising tobacco haze, and say, 'You framed me for murder, bastard. You had everything fixed ... except the jury. That jury blew it. And, you've sweat bricks, ever since.'

CHAPTER FIFTY-ONE

He's licked. I've done it!

Oh, he fights on; a man like Crawford doesn't fold up quite as easy as *that*—he bluffs, he dodges, he feints ... but these tactics don't alter the basic fact that he's licked.

It shows on the parched lips. It shows on the slight sheen of perspiration which covers the face. It shows in the knotting and unknotting of the restless fingers. It shows in the voice; a voice which, for the first time, lacks the certainty—the subtle, sardonic overtone—of the true 'Crawford' manner of speech.

I smile across at him. Not with arrogance. Not with

triumph. Not even with satisfaction. If anything, with a touch of compassion ... perhaps even pity.

'Satisfied?' I ask, quietly.

'It has holes in it.' He treats me to a quick, twisted, but rather weary smile. 'Too many holes to hold water.'

'I'm a builder,' I remind him. 'I can mend a leaking cauldron ... no sweat.'

'Really? It—er—interests me.'

'You have friends.'

'We all have friends, Russell.'

'True. But, some of your friends shouldn't *be* friends.'

He waits for it and, truth to tell, this is my biggest gamble of all. I stand, or fall flat on my face, with what I'm going to say next. With how I say it ... and whether I'm right. If I'm right, he's finished. If I'm wrong, he can laugh in my face and tell me to go screw myself.

I send up a quick prayer.

I meet him, eye-for-eye, and say, 'Three friends. Tearaways. Killers. Jim, John ... and the name of the third isn't important.'

'Very common names,' he whispers.

'Your friends.'

'That's what *you* say.'

'That's what *they* say,' I lie.

'Is ... that ... a ... fact?'

The words are forced past his stiffened lips, one at a time. There is a pause, between each word. Each word threatens to choke him. Each word is a curse upon three men he thought he controlled.

I keep a rock-straight face, but I know. I have hit the gold ... plumb centre.

I say, 'They bounced me around, Crawford. They gave me this.' I moved my gloved hand. I continue, 'It's a thing I don't like ... being bounced around. So-o, I dug a few holes, and out popped a trio of worms. Greedy worms. They know the value of money—and I have

181

money, Crawford ... one hell of a lot more money than you'll *ever* have.'

'So?'

'You're nailed to a cross, friend ... that's the "so". I'm prepared to purchase the nails and the hammer. Your bully-boy mates are prepared to drive the nails home. They'll go down—sure they'll go down ... like I was supposed to go down. But, when they come out, they'll be rich men. When you come out, you'll be nothing. Nothing!'

He watches my face—scrutinises my expression—searching for some tiny weakness which he can use to his own advantage. He sees nothing ... because I make damn sure he sees nothing.

He finishes the Drambuie left in his glass, pours out another inch, or so, picks up the glass, pushes himself from the armchair and walks to the window. It is dusk, beyond the glass and the panes form black mirrors through which he can see an inverted image of the room.

He talks to the image. Soft talk. Bent talk. The talk of a man who has never truly understood what the word 'honesty' means.

He murmurs, 'Okay, Russell. Name the deal.'

It is, I suppose, the nearest thing he has ever come to complete capitulation ... but he has some way to go, yet.

I turn my head, and watch his face, through the reflecting pane.

'The deal,' he repeats, grimly. 'There has to be a deal in these things. There's *always* a deal. I'm waiting.'

'Life?' I suggest. 'The deal you offered me? Twenty years ... or thereabouts?'

'No, no.' He shakes his head, with absolute conviction. 'This isn't a revenge act. Those germs you mentioned. What they have is for sale, and you have money. If this was a vendetta, you could have had me buried, by now.'

I lean sideways in the chair and switch on a stand-lamp to counter the mounting gloom. The shaded light makes the window darker and, in doing so, picks out details of his reflection. The tiny furrow of worry, between his eyes. The tightened muscles at his mouth corners. The face of a man who, until this moment, knew all the answers ... but who now isn't even too sure of the questions.

'I know Roebuck,' he says, and the remark is in the nature of an offer.

'A nonentity,' I murmur. 'He won't be with us long.'

'A word from me, and the firm ...'

'The firm, too,' I interrupt, harshly. 'It's finished. A spent squib. Kelly—y'know Kelly? ... ex-cop, now private investigator?'

'I know Kelly.'

'He's handling Roebuck. Personally. On my instructions. On my cheque. The firm goes ... it's rotten, it's what it deserves. Roebuck goes with it. What's left of Roebuck, even the worms won't touch.'

He moves his head in a tiny sideways jerk; a half-nod which is accompanied by a quick and twisted smile.

He says, 'You know how to hate, Russell.'

'I've learned ... fast.'

'It's self-destructive. Unless, of course, it's controlled.'

'Mine,' I assure him, grimly, 'is running riot.'

'So-o ... no deal.' He turns from the window, and adds, 'So, what comes next?'

I motion to a side-table. On the side-table there is a telephone.

I say, 'One of two things, Crawford. There's no third option ... just the two. You go down for life. No "ifs". No "buts". No "maybes". You have a cell for a home, for a long, long time ... that I promise.'

'And the alternative?'

'Pick up the phone. Dial a number. Get somebody here —in this cottage ... make it a nice, cosy threesome. Get the right person. Get that person here, before midnight.

And maybe—*maybe*—you'll still be a detective chief inspector at this time tomorrow.'

He walks to the phone. Sips the Drambuie. Places the glass alongside the instrument, sighs, then lifts the receiver.

CHAPTER FIFTY-TWO

I should feel happy. At least triumphant. I should be on top of the world, because this is what I've worked for, and this is what I've prayed for, and this is what I now have.

Instead, I feel nothing. Nothing! No sadness, no pity, no elation, no satisfaction ... *nothing*.

They each sit in an armchair and listen, while I talk. I stand, feet planted firmly on the hearthrug, and I voice my thoughts and, sometimes, I ask a question and, when I ask a question the question is answered, without hesitation. There are no more secrets. No more hiding places. No more anything.

The truth is out ... and the truth stinks to high heaven.

It is five minutes to midnight. Five minutes to a new day. Five minutes to the first day of the rest of my life ... and one hell of a life it promises to be!

'What was her name?' I ask.

'Pauline. Pauline Knopf ... she had mid-European blood in her.'

His answer is quiet and unhurried.

'A nurse. That's what you said—a nurse ... right?'

'Not a very good nurse. She grew pregnant.'

'You, of course, being the proud father-to-be.'

'No. The proud father *not*-to-be,' he corrects me.

I glance at her, as he makes the smart-Aleck come-back and, for a moment, I see what might be mistaken for contempt touch her mouth and eyes.

'She had to—er—"disappear", of course,' I say.

'Of course,' he agrees. 'She was becoming an embarrassment.'

'And you wanted my wife.'

'I already *had* your wife.' He treats himself to a quick, tight smile. 'I merely wanted to *keep* your wife.'

'A pity,' I murmur.

'I think so, too.'

'No ... I mean for the unfortunate Miss Knopf.'

'Ye-es, I suppose so. For her, too.'

'She had to die.'

'What else? What other certain way?'

'Why here?' I ask.

He nods towards the other armchair, and murmurs, 'Her idea. Very private. And, of course, ideal for other reasons.'

'Of course,' I agree.

'I introduced her as my sister,' he explains.

'Your *rich* sister, I hope.'

'Rolling in it.'

'Why the hell can't you two ...' she begins.

'*Shut up!*' I waste no time on pleasantries. I snarl, 'Just sit there, and listen. You've a lot to learn yet, sweetheart. Call it extra-mural education ... and put it down to experience.'

I turn to him, and say, 'The three goons, of course?'

He nods, amiably.

'Did it take three of them to hold her down? To strip her, and re-clothe her?'

'Two ... and her, of course.'

'It must have been quite a scene. Quite a performance.'

He says, 'One kept watch, by the telephone kiosk about a mile up the lane. He sent the hoax call. On my way here, I dipped the headlights a couple of times. He phoned the cottage ... gave everybody time to get clear.'

'Everybody?'

'All except ...' He stops. Chuckles, gently. It is a madman's chuckle, which sends spiders scurrying up my spine. He says, 'Y'know, Russell, there's a curl to the tail of this story. You'll appreciate it. The post-mortem—it was one of those false alarm jobs ... she *wasn't* pregnant, after all.'

'So-o ... all for nothing?'

'It's one way of looking at it,' he smiles.

'And nice timing, too.'

'Not too difficult. We knew where you'd be ... the site. We knew you'd follow your daily routine ... stay there, until knocking-off time. We'd timed the distance, from the site to the cottage. Short of a blow-out—an engine failure—we could estimate your time of arrival.'

'And the gun?' I ask.

'We left it handy. You picked it up ... what else? The most natural action in the world.'

'And, there I was, *flagrante delicto* ... as the saying goes.'

'As the saying goes,' he agrees. He smiles, then muses, 'Y'know, it must be very unusual. Unique, almost. A copper investigating a murder he himself has committed.'

'*And* detecting it,' I add, wrily.

'Neat,' he admits.

'But,' I say, gently, 'with certain loose ends dangling around in the breeze.'

'Such as?'

'The heavies. *They* still know.'

'They're professionals. Officially, they'll have forgotten it, already.'

'Crawford,' I accuse, 'you don't read your crime reports very carefully.'

'Eh?'

'Unless there's been a rail strike, between here and Hell, they're already handling pitchforks.'

'Oh!'

The shock hits him like a runaway locomotive. It drives the colour from his cheeks. It brings a momentary look of panic into his eyes.

'They're dead,' I amplify. '*Very* dead.'

He says, 'Oh!' again. There doesn't seem much else for him to say.

That being the case, *I* talk. I talk hard and tough. I mean every word I say, and I wish it to be clearly understood that I *do* mean every word I say. I stare at the hearthrug—at a point in the pattern, a little way in from my feet—and I let the words come, as they filter through my mind. Freely, softly, but very deliberately and with absolute finality. There is no chronological order. It is not necessary. This is not a dénouement. We all know the answers ... every answer.

This is merely a reminding of those facts, plus an ultimatum.

I say, 'Some people cry very readily. Even men. But not men like Bill Macks. And Bill Macks is weeping ... and I doubt if he will ever stop weeping. He is a broken man. Broken in health—broken in spirit ... and the only wish he has is for the grave. I've seen him a couple of times. I have no desire to see him again. He represents a part of me. Something ... a part of me I didn't know, and hoped I didn't have.

'We built a firm—Bill Macks, and I—a firm which, in effect was a monument to simple honesty. And that firm's gone. The monument has been demolished ... and, I suspect, by someone in this room. Roebuck ... who the hell cares for the Roebucks of this world. They're harmless. They have no teeth ... unless, and until, somebody *gives* them teeth. The go-between. The bastard—the bitch —who can listen to one, and get at the other. Bill weakened. He was got at, and he knows he was got at ... and the knowledge has broken his heart. It's killing him, inch at a time.

'It's a form of murder. As murderous as what happened here, in this room, on Twelfth Night. A woman, shot to death, in my home. With bullets shot from my gun. And then the switch.

'As a senior copper—as the man in charge of the investigation—you could fix it. Nobody else could have done it but, with you it was easy. You wanted rid of your nurse. You rid yourself of your nurse ... then framed me, to stand in the dock, accused of the crime. You directed operations. You gave all the orders. Wrong orders—carefully thought-out orders—to make sure none of the men working under you asked the wrong questions of the wrong people.

'You did it for two reasons. To get rid of a woman you'd tired of. To free a woman you wanted. You damn-near did it, too. You knew the tough-babies ... it's your job to know them. You approached them, you paid them, then you gave yourself a great alibi. Not too involved ... but fool-proof. I pleaded "Not Guilty", for a very fundamental reason. Because I *wasn't* guilty. It's what you expected ... but you were sure enough to think my plea didn't matter. But—something you should know, Crawford—a remand in custody, week after week, gives a man time to think. That cell ... I worked things out, in the solitude of that cell. Not everything. But enough. It had to be one of two people ... you, or Bill Macks. But not Bill Macks—I decided that, within the first forty-eight hours. You don't know Vi. Vi would have killed *him*. So, it had to be *you*.

'First job, then, was to place my trust in God and the jury system. And it worked ... much to your disgust. Second job, was to throw you ... to give you the last thing on earth you expected. A *confession*. I wonder what the hell went through your mind, Crawford, when I admitted to a killing *you'd* committed? I wonder how well you slept that night.

'Then, I engaged Kelly. First, for the murder *and* the corruption, then—because Kelly had enough police-sense

188

to realise that the two things might *not* be connected—just for the corruption. To blast Roebuck into outer-space, for what he'd done to Bill Macks.

'The killing—the frame-up—was a very personal thing. A thing between you and me.

'I made mistakes. I earned myself a hospital-sized thumping ... but even that proved something. That you knew it had happened—you, who are so uninterested in what goes on outside your own manor, that you don't even know about a triple-killing—you knew all about Harvey Russell being taught a very sharp and very rough lesson. You came to see me. Not about my health ... but to double-check that they'd done a good job, and that I couldn't name them.'

I stare at the carpet for a while, in silence.

Then, I continue, 'I don't like having the boot put in, Crawford. I retaliate. I get very cross. I had to shoot one of 'em. Then, I had to shoot the other two, to remove witnesses ... the sort of logic you'll, no doubt, understand. That makes me a three-times killer, friend. Two up, on you, in fact. *And,* the police have the whole wide world to choose from. Who knows? ... some other unfortunate might have to put his trust in twelve good men and true.' I raise my eyes from the hearthrug, look into his face, and say, 'Now, that's really *funny,* Crawford. Don't you think? A confession—and, this time, a genuine one-hundred-per-cent confession—and you can't do a damn thing about it. Touch it. Breathe on it too heavily, and your own house of cards comes tumbling down, to mix with mine.'

'We—er—made a mistake,' he says, quietly.

I nod.

'Where?'

I turn towards the other armchair, and say, 'The hand. The right hand—open, palm-upwards ... if you please.'

She obeys, like a sleepwalker.

I nod at the tiny scar, and say, It was missing. The fist

189

was clenched. The fire didn't touch it. In the morgue—
as far back as *that*—I knew I was dealing with jiggery-
pokery.'

'So bloody simple,' sighs Crawford.

'They tell me,' I say, sardonically, 'that, even at the
Crucifixion, some thieving hound stole the fourth nail. You
can be sure of nothing, in this world.

'But I was sure it was Lissa's body I'd seen here, in this
cottage. *You'd* convinced me. Then—at the morgue—I
knew I'd been conned. I was shocked—but, more than
that, I was curious ... and bloody annoyed. I'd been
framed. At that time, I thought I'd been framed for the
murder of my wife—then, for the murder of some unknown woman, guyed up as my wife—as a cover-up for the
back-handers. A very personal thing. A very private thing.
And—big laugh here, Crawford—a thing I thought you'd
refuse to believe ... that it wasn't Lissa's body, after all.
You could prove it *was*. All I could do was *say* it wasn't.
And I didn't feel like wasting too much time arguing. I
wanted a head on a charger ... fast! What I didn't want
was weeks—months—of wrangling with officialdom ...
so-o, I played along with the gag. They say luck favours
the fools of this world. It favoured me, that day. To have
told you—*you* of all people—that Lissa wasn't dead
would have really set me up for target practice.'

'Nevertheless,' he smiles, 'Mexican stand-off. We can
each trump the other's ace. So ... where do we go from
here?'

'You go back to your game of cops-and-robbers,' I say,
harshly. 'She stays with me. She's my wife ... she *stays*
my wife. But, this time, there are certain rules. She behaves
herself. Immaculately. One wrong word—one wrong
action—and I belt the living hell out of her ... and enjoy
doing it. And with complete safety. Because, the last
person she'll yell for is a bobby.'

CHAPTER FIFTY-THREE

And that's it.

Man and wife—murderer and murderess—outwardly respectable people, living in a very respectable neighbourhood. We've changed our names, of course ... even our Christian names. We loathe each other, but that particular feeling we keep well under wraps.

We are, I suppose, a little scared of each other. The first murder is always the worst. But, to date, we live our own comfortable hate-filled lives; walking, as if on broken eggshells; wondering what the hell goes on in the other's mind.

Nevertheless, we survive ... and the great secret of our survival is mutual distrust.

Who am I?

What name do I live under?

We-ell, now ...

Next time you see a neighbour washing his car—mowing his lawn—putting a lick of paint on the woodwork of his property ... pause a while.

Just give it a very careful second thought.

Who knows? ... it could be *me*!